BOUNTY FLIGHT

CEDAR CREEK SUSPENSE, VOLUME 2

VIOLET HOWE

www.violethowe.com

Cover Design: Elizabeth Mackey
www.elizabethmackeygraphics.com

Published by Charbar Productions, LLC
(v1)

Print ISBN: 978-1-7327269-5-6
BN Print ISBN: 9798765538494
Ebook ISBN: 978-1-7327269-4-9

For Tawdra

For road trips and late night roomie talks, for inside jokes and sisterhood, for support and guidance through tears and laughter, for Dolly Parton and Cat Missouri, for the right kind of Almond Joyous, and much, much more.

Thanks for being willing to brave nightmares and phobias for me. In more ways than one.

BOOKS BY VIOLET HOWE

Tales Behind the Veils

Diary of a Single Wedding Planner

Diary of a Wedding Planner in Love

Diary of an Engaged Wedding Planner

Maggie

The Cedar Creek Collection

Cedar Creek Mysteries:

The Ghost in the Curve

The Glow in the Woods

The Phantom in the Footlights

Cedar Creek Families:

Building Fences

Crossing Paths

Cedar Creek Suspense:

Whiskey Flight

Bounty Flight

Soul Sisters at Cedar Mountain Lodge

Christmas Sisters

Christmas Hope

Christmas Peace

Visit www.violethowe.com to subscribe to Violet's monthly newsletter for news on upcoming releases, events, sales, and other tidbits.

ONE

I have no memory of the moment the plane slammed into the ground.

I lost consciousness at some point prior to impact. When I awoke, still in some semblance of the brace position with my head between my knees, I didn't know what had happened at first. All I knew was I couldn't breathe.

A heavy weight lay across my back, pressing my chest against my thighs. My bag was squashed between my legs and my rib cage, leaving my lungs no room to expand. Disoriented panic set in as I pushed against the unyielding weight, and my brain seemed to short circuit, sputtering little flashes of memory that made no sense at first.

The smell of lavender hand lotion. A woman praying. The sky where it shouldn't be. A man cursing. Flames. Blood-curdling screams and the horrific crunch of metal. And beneath it all played the flight attendants' continual chant of *"brace, brace, brace."*

But then my mind locked on a memory of the clearest crystal-blue eyes I'd ever seen, and suddenly, it was as though a film reel loaded into my mind's projector, and the events leading up to the crash played back at warp speed.

I'd first noticed those blue eyes when he arrived at the departure gate. As usual, my nose was buried in a book, but something made me look up. Almost like the universe had silently called to me and said, *"Girl, you don't want to miss this."*

He approached the gate with two other men, but he might as well have been the only person in the entire terminal, because he was all I saw.

He was six-three, maybe four, and built like he knew his way around a gym but didn't live there. He walked with a confident swagger, his fists by his sides and his narrowed eyes scanning the crowd as though he was looking for trouble and hoping he found it.

His entire demeanor screamed *badass*, and suddenly, I no longer doubted the validity of the book heroines who fall in love at first sight. Or in lust, at the very least. Never had my body reacted to a stranger with such immediate attraction, and I tingled with such intensity I squirmed in my seat.

Our gazes locked and a jolt of electricity shot straight through me. His eyes widened a bit and a hint of a smile played at the corner of his mouth. For a moment, I thought perhaps he'd felt it too, but then common sense reminded me how ridiculous that was, and my cheeks heated as I looked away. He was more likely smiling because I was staring at him like a starstruck teenager, desire blatant on my face.

I tried to refocus on my book, but the story no longer held my interest. When I couldn't help but venture another peek, he stood at the desk between the two men. His tie-wearing companion leaned forward to speak with the attendant in hushed tones, pulling something from his wallet to show her. The third man stood off to the side, shifting his weight from foot to foot, his hands shoved in his back pockets. He was much younger than the other two, younger than me even. Barely early twenties, if that. With a face so pale it was almost green and eyes that darted back and forth in a constant scan of his surroundings, he looked as though he might throw up at any moment.

They were an intriguing trio, but my attention was caught by the one in the center. The one who had sent my pulse racing with nothing more than a glance.

Broad shoulders stretched the cotton of his black T-shirt taut across his back, and as he rested his palm on the desk, I admired the definition of the muscles in his forearms and the bulge of his bicep where it disappeared beneath the shirt's sleeve. My gaze continued to drift down to his tapered waist and the snug hug of his jeans, but then he shifted his weight and began to turn. I forced my eyes back to the pages of my book, not wanting to be caught openly ogling him again.

After re-reading the same paragraph three times without comprehending the words, I looked up again, determined to appear casual. The ruse of nonchalance disappeared the moment I realized he'd gone, and I sat up and turned left to right in a desperate search for any sight of him.

Where the hell had he gone so quickly? And why did I care?

His absence left me melancholy, which was absurd. I didn't even know the guy and never would! What did it matter? It wasn't like I would have struck up a conversation with him if he'd stayed, even if I had somehow been afforded the opportunity. What was I going to do? Walk up uninvited and introduce myself? Give him my number like we were in a club on singles night rather than surrounded by travelers in an airport? Any guy that gorgeous was likely already attached. Or a total player who kept a bevy of ladies on speed dial.

I tried to tell myself it was ridiculous to pine over some guy just because of his appearance, even if he did look like a long-lost Hemsworth brother they'd somehow managed to hide from the world. Looks only went so far, and he could be a total jerk for all I knew. The handsome ones often were.

But that didn't keep me from watching for his return, even after I'd boarded the flight. As each new passenger made their way down the aisle toward me, my disappointment grew, and when they'd finally shut the door to the cabin, I lost all hope.

For the first part of the flight, I spent way too much time indulging my thoughts of him. *Who was he? What did he do for a living? Did he live in the Central Florida area like me, or was he just one of the thousands of visitors who passed through the Orlando airport every day?*

Without any concrete answers, I filled in the blanks with whatever I wanted, and by the time the flight attendants began serving refreshments, I'd concocted quite the hero in my head. I'd even imagined us a newly-rewritten beginning and a happily-ever-after ending.

The bottle of water I'd brought on the plane was empty and my bladder was full, and I knew if I didn't make a run for the lavatory before the refreshment cart got to my row, I'd be blocked from going until they finished their journey down the aisle.

I strapped the small backpack I was using as a travel purse onto my chest and stood to begin walking toward the back of the plane. I'd only gone a few rows when I spotted him, and I stopped short in the aisle in disbelief.

No way! This was impossible!

He'd disappeared before they even called for boarding to begin, and I'd watched every single passenger who'd gone down the gateway before me or who boarded the plane after me. He'd been nowhere in sight. Yet, here he was, seated on the aisle in the back row of the plane with an empty seat between him and the guy who'd looked nauseated.

Could he have boarded the plane before anyone else? If so, how had I not noticed him when I got on and came to my seat?

The two men leaned toward each other talking, but then the lost Hemsworth turned to look at me as if he'd sensed my stare.

The jolt hit again as our eyes locked, and then he smiled—a breathtaking, dazzling smile that made my knees go weak.

Damn! Could he feel that too? He had to. How could he not with the way his eyes lit up?

The woman next to me cleared her throat, and I realized I had grabbed the back of her seat to brace myself.

Embarrassed, I continued to move forward down the aisle, but I didn't dare break eye contact. I'd found him again after thinking he was lost to me forever, and I intended to spend every available second taking in his perfection to memorize every detail.

He never looked away as I approached, and the intensity of his gaze sent goose bumps rippling across my skin. Only when I'd passed by him and slid the lavatory door shut did I release the breath I'd been holding.

My dark brown eyes seemed brighter than usual as they stared back at me from the mirror, and my cheeks were pink with a rosy flush.

It was ridiculous to be this worked up over a complete stranger, and yet, my mind was scheming to figure out a way to talk to him. Unless I wanted to make a fool of myself standing in the aisle with an out-of-the-blue introduction, my best chance wouldn't be until baggage claim, but I decided to spruce up a bit for the walk back since I was certain he'd be watching.

I pulled a tube of lip gloss from my bag and dabbed it across my bottom lip, careful not to apply too much and make the effort obvious. As I pressed my lips together to rub it in, I fluffed my hair with my fingers, thankful for the morning's low humidity that had kept it from frizzing, and then I turned my attention to taking care of necessary business.

A rumble vibrated beneath me, but I assumed it was simply one of those odd sounds planes make. At the time, I was more concerned with balancing my hover inside the tiny lavatory as I fought to get the toilet paper holder to release more than one sheet at a time.

The plane rumbled again as I finished rinsing my hands. I crinkled my nose at the soap's lingering antiseptic smell, and once I'd dried my hands with a paper towel, I pulled a small tube of lavender hand lotion from my bag.

I stood rubbing a dollop into my skin when a deafening boom filled the air, followed by a horribly piercing screech that seemed to tear straight through my eardrums. Crying out in both shock and pain, I clamped my hands over my ears, but that left me completely unprepared to catch myself as the plane rolled to the left, tossing me against the wall of the lavatory.

Frantic to escape the tiny space, I jerked the door open and rushed into the galley with my ears still ringing and my heart pounding. Before I could get my bearings, the plane shuddered again with a drastic drop in altitude, leaving my body momentarily suspended in weightlessness before tossing me back down at the end of the aisle between the back rows.

I reached for the nearest armrest, desperate to find some measure of stability, but then movement caught my eye in the aisle ahead of me and I looked up in horror as the massive beverage cart barreled toward me. I scrambled to try and stand but stumbled, and then a muscular arm clamped around my waist like a vice grip, lifting me up and out of the way seconds before the cart crashed into the armrest I'd been clinging to.

The arm around my waist loosened its grip as the plane leveled, and before my mind even registered that I was sitting in the lost Hemsworth's lap, he had lifted me again and shoved me into the empty seat next to him.

"Fasten your seatbelt," he shouted over the chaotic din of screaming in the cabin.

I did as he said without question, and as I clicked the seat belt in place, a flight attendant stood at the front of the aisle and called for calm over the loudspeaker.

In soothing tones, she assured us there was no need for panic, but her appearance wasn't exactly reassuring. Blood seeped from a small cut above her eyebrow, and her hand trembled as she smoothed it over her disheveled hair.

Judging by how fast the screams died down, some of the passengers must have believed her spiel, but not everyone was convinced.

"What the hell was that?" asked the man who had accompanied the lost Hemsworth onto the plane. "We gonna crash, ain't we? We gonna die." He groaned and looked past me to his traveling companion. "I ain't wanting to die today, man. I can't go out this way. I told you I was terrified of flying."

"You're not dying today, Kirby," my rescuer said, his voice as deep and rich as I had imagined it might be. "You have a date with a judge, and nothing will stop me from making sure you're there for it."

I stared at the lost Hemsworth in a bewildered state of shock. Moments before, I'd begged the universe to give us a way to meet, but bodily injury and fearing for my life wasn't what I had in mind.

"You okay?" he asked, staring back at me. He seemed completely unfazed, as if airplanes fell apart around him all the time.

"I, uh, I think so." My shoulder ached, my knees stung with carpet burn, and a pain radiated from the side of my head, but all things considered, it could have been worse. "Thanks. For, uh, you know, rescuing me. Um, picking me up. So, yeah. Thanks."

My words tumbled over each other as my brain struggled to process everything that had just happened.

"No problem," he said with a slight nod and a hint of a smile.

I couldn't stop staring at him, and I marveled at the fact that even in the midst of a near-death experience, I could still be affected by the unexpected close proximity to what had to be the most gorgeous man I'd ever seen in my life.

He tilted his head to one side and his eyes narrowed. "You sure you're all right? You took a pretty hard tumble, and you seem dazed."

"Yeah." I nodded. "I think I am. All right, I mean. And maybe a little dazed."

The flight attendant announced they'd be coming through the cabin to attend to injuries, and I turned from my rescuer to do a quick scan of my surroundings, which appeared to be returning to normal.

"My name's Lauryn, by the way," I said when I looked back at him. Part of me was shocked that I could even consider making small talk under the circumstances, but another more adventurous part of me figured if the universe had gone to all this trouble to present the opportunity, I'd better not waste it.

He shook my extended hand and released it. "Brick."

"Brick? Really?" My incredulous tone sounded rude even to me, and I rushed to explain in case I'd offended him. "I mean, that's a cool name. Interesting, for sure. I've never known anyone named Brick. Is it a family name?"

"Damn, look how close the trees are," Kirby said, his forehead pressed to the window. "We must have fallen pretty far. Why ain't we climbing back up?"

I leaned toward the window and craned my neck to see past him, drawing back in alarm with the realization that we were barely above the tree-covered mountaintops.

"Why *are* we flying so low?" I asked, turning back to Brick as though he would somehow have the answers.

"I bet we lost an engine," Kirby said before Brick could respond. "Probably hit a bird. They say a single bird can bring down a big jet like this. They fly into the engine and then bam! Down we go. We're probably down to one engine now."

He let out a stream of curses and jerked his hand against the seat rest with a loud rattle. The jacket that had been laid across his lap fell away, and my eyes widened at the sight of handcuffs securing him to the seat.

"You gotta let me outta these, man," he said to Brick. "If we're going down, I need my hands. I won't have a chance in hell in surviving if you don't let me loose, bro."

Brick's voice was gruff and firm. "That's not happening."

"This is ridiculous. Where the hell am I gonna go?"

Brick leaned his head back and clasped his hands together over his waist, the surreal epitome of a calm, relaxed state. "I told you I need some sleep, and I'm not taking any chances with you."

Kirby jerked harder at the handcuffs with another stream of curses, and suddenly, I had to question the sanity of remaining next to him just to talk to a guy. Even if the guy did look like he could be a legit Greek god.

"I think maybe I should go back to my seat." I reached to unbuckle my seat belt.

"I'd stay put for a little longer if I were you," Brick said. "The captain hasn't turned off the seat belt sign, and I wouldn't bet on us being out of the woods just yet."

I frowned but left the seat belt buckled. "What do you mean? You think we're still in danger?"

Brick shrugged. "All I know is something pretty big broke off back there, something important enough that losing it damned near sent us to the ground. Obviously, they've regained some measure of control, but we haven't picked up what we lost in speed or altitude since it happened. I'd say we've got a pretty serious issue they're trying to figure out how to address."

"But the flight attendant said everything's okay."

He raised an eyebrow and cocked his head slightly. "Not exactly. She said everyone should remain calm and that there was no need to panic, which is what she's supposed to say to keep people from losing their shit in an emergency."

TWO

I looked for the attendant, eager for any clue as to whether she seemed concerned. She was at the front of the plane, cradling the phone headset against her ear. Her head was bandaged and her hair had been combed, but deep frown lines creased her forehead as she listened to what I assumed must be someone in the cockpit on the other end of the line.

The other two attendants were making their way down the aisle, stopping at every row to inquire about injuries and ask passengers to remain calm and stay buckled. They both wore ever-present, reassuring smiles, and I clung to the hope that their unconcerned demeanor meant we were okay.

When the male attendant reached us, he took a moment to secure the errant beverage cart back in the galley before returning with his smile firmly in place.

"Everyone okay here? Any injuries to report?"

"What the hell happened?" Kirby asked.

Kirby wasn't the first passenger to ask, and in a ridiculously upbeat voice considering the gravity of his words, the attendant repeated the same answer he'd obviously given multiple times as he approached us. He had perfected it almost to the point of sounding robotic.

"We're experiencing a mechanical issue, but there's no need to panic. The captain will give us an update momentarily. In the meantime, please remain seated with your seatbelts fastened."

"I should probably return to my seat," I said, unbuckling the belt. "I was in the restroom when…whatever that was happened, and this was the closest empty spot."

His smile did falter then, and he glanced over his shoulder toward the other attendant, who was assisting an emotional elderly passenger. He looked back at Brick instead of me and the robotic tone was gone from his voice. "Would you mind if she sat here a while longer? I know you're required to have the entire row, but we need to keep the aisles clear and have everyone stay seated."

"Sure," Brick said with a slight shrug of one shoulder. "That's no problem."

The attendant's smile returned as he looked at me. "Why don't you stay here until the captain says it's safe to move? Then you can return to your seat."

I glanced at Kirby's handcuffs and back to the attendant, but his attention had shifted to his colleague. She'd finished her phone conversation and was making her way toward us at a clipped pace. The other attendants fell in step behind her as she led them to the back galley.

I leaned forward to get a view of them as they chatted, and though I couldn't hear their words, my stomach sank as I watched the tension play out across their faces. Something was wrong. Terribly wrong.

"You wanna switch seats? Need me to move?"

Brick's deep voice so close to my ear startled me. I hadn't realized how far over him I'd leaned in my attempt to hear the attendants, and warmth crept into my cheeks as I sat back flat against my seat.

"Sorry. I was trying to hear what she was saying. She was talking with someone on the phone and then she came to talk to the other attendants, so she must know what's happening."

"I'll tell you what's happening," Kirby said, his voice frantic as he sat staring out the window. "We're gonna die. That's what's happening. Look how close the trees are now!"

The sun hung so low in the sky it was on the verge of disappearing behind the mountains, but the dim setting light revealed we were nearly skimming the tips of the treetops.

My heart still hadn't calmed from the last scare, and it began to pound again in earnest as I leaned forward to look at the attendants, still huddled in the galley whispering.

"Why aren't they telling us anything? Why aren't we climbing back up?"

Brick glanced over his shoulder at them and then looked past Kirby and me toward the trees. He sighed and leaned his head back against the seat, closing his eyes as he folded his hands in his lap again. "They'll tell us what we need to know when we need to know it."

How could he be so calm?

I was sitting there with my heart about to come out of my chest and every nerve in my body on high alert, and he looked like he was ready for a nap.

"You can't possibly be planning to sleep at a time like this," I said.

His eyes remained closed. "Why not? Worrying won't help the situation, and since I'm not a pilot or a mechanic, I can't fly the plane or fix the problem."

"But you are a cop, right? You could go ask them what's going on. They'd probably tell you."

"He ain't no cop," Kirby scoffed.

"What are you then?" I asked Brick. "DEA? An air marshal?"

Before Brick could answer, Kirby laughed. "He wishes he was an air marshal. He's just a low-life bounty hunter."

Immediately, my mind ran through a mental inventory of books, television, and movies for any characters in that role, and I had to admit, it was a good fit for him.

"You're a bounty hunter? Really?"

His eyes still remained closed. "Fugitive recovery agent."

"Which is just a fancy way of saying he's a bounty hunter," Kirby said, leaning in closer to me. He inhaled deeply and smiled. "Damn, you smell nice."

Before I even had time to draw back away from him, Brick sprang forward to reach across me and twist his fist in Kirby's T-shirt.

"Give her space and get against the window, now," he growled.

Kirby complied with a scowl, pressing his back to the window wall. "I didn't do anything. Damn, man. You need to lighten up."

"You don't speak to her again; do you hear me?" Brick released Kirby's shirt and looked at me, his eyes still narrowed. "Are you all right?"

"I'm fine," I said, shocked more by the swiftness of his reaction and the gruffness of his voice than the original comment. I wondered what Kirby had done to be handcuffed and in Brick's custody. Was he dangerous? I considered again that perhaps I should try to return to my original seat.

The hum of the intercom drew my attention as the captain cleared his throat and began to speak in a somber tone.

"This is your captain speaking. As you may have surmised, we've had an unexpected mechanical issue, and the plane has suffered some damage. Pretty substantial, I'm sorry to say. We're going to need to cut our flight short and find a place where we can get down as quickly and safely as possible."

I looked to the window, where the treetops now appeared even closer than before. Kirby turned from looking out to meet my eyes, and I knew we were likely both thinking the same thing.

How on earth were we going to land a plane in this terrain?

"I'm not going to sugarcoat it," the captain continued. "This won't be a smooth landing. We're going to try to set down in a lake that's just up ahead."

A lake? We were landing in a lake?

As if on cue, the flight attendants emerged from the galley, and they sought to quiet the rising quell as the captain finished speaking.

"Our crew will assist you with preparing for a water landing," he said. "I ask that you please remain calm and obey their instructions so we can have the best possible outcome."

The best possible outcome? We were crash landing in a lake in the middle of nowhere. There didn't seem to be a best outcome, and my breath quickened as fear seized my heart.

The attendant nearest us began instructions on how to use the seat as a flotation device and the mechanics of a proper brace position.

The words didn't compute in my head. They sounded warped, like an audiobook played back on too slow of a speed.

I looked to Brick; his eyes were open and sharply focused on the male attendant as he spoke.

"You gotta unlock me, man," Kirby's voice had taken on a new sense of urgency as he pled with Brick. "What if I need to swim? How am I gonna swim if I'm handcuffed to the seat?"

Swim? Oh my God! Would we need to swim?

They'd spoken of rafts and inflatable life jackets, but somehow, my brain had refused to compute what that really meant. We were pretty high up in the mountains, and it was barely spring. How cold would the water be? Knowing it would be warm when I landed in Florida, I'd opted for a thin dress, bare legs, and heeled sandals. I wasn't dressed for swimming, especially not in frigid water.

Besides, what if the water rushed in so suddenly that I couldn't reach an exit? What if I was knocked unconscious and then trapped beneath the surface? Even if I survived the initial impact of the plane hitting the water, I could still drown without ever making it out, especially since I was in the very back row.

My assigned seat was just in front of the wing, only a couple of rows from the emergency exit. If I'd still been there, I'd have a much better chance of escaping. Instead, I was at the back of the plane, trapped between a presumed dangerous fugitive and a hunk of a guy who seemed to be completely unconcerned by our circumstances. Should I try to stand and make it back to my seat? Would it make a difference?

Kirby's pleas grew louder, and Brick swore beneath his breath and told him to knock it off as he reached into his front pocket and pulled out a set of keys. Reaching across me, he unlocked the cuff on Kirby's right hand and freed him from the armrest, but his grip on Kirby's wrist tightened so much that Kirby winced and let out an expletive.

"You try anything—anything at all—and I promise you that this plane going down will be the least of your concerns."

I shuddered at the coldness of Brick's voice and wondered again what the hell Kirby had done. If he was such a threat, why was there only one man guarding him?

My situation was perilous enough with the malfunctioning plane attempting an emergency landing. I didn't care to add the desperate acts of a dangerous criminal to my risk factor.

"I think I'm going to try and make it back to my seat," I started to say, but before I could finish the sentence, the plane wobbled, and the attendants commanded us to assume the brace position and began their chant.

The entire situation went to another level of terrifying as I bent forward and prepared to die. My initial thoughts were consumed with my family, but it hurt too much to consider that I might never see them again. I tried to turn to a different page in my mind, and unfortunately, that led me to consider how cold the water was going to be and whether it was going to hurt when we hit. Fear turned to panic, and I began to hyperventilate, my breaths too quick and too shallow to be effective. The lack of oxygen combined with a terror like nothing I'd ever experienced made me dizzy, and I squeezed my eyes shut so tightly it hurt.

"Lauryn," Brick said, pressing his knee to mine. "Look at me."

My eyes popped open to find his handsome face only inches from mine as we sat folded over, headed to our death. In my hysteria, I almost laughed at the absurdity of it all. Why did it have to happen this way? Was fate's sense of humor so incredibly twisted that I'd be introduced to my ideal man and have him set off sparks inside me only to have our story end before its first chapter could even begin?

"You have to stay calm so you can be alert, okay?" His voice remained quiet and steady despite the chaos unfolding around us. "You need to be able to think fast and act quickly. Here, purse your lips, like this." He puckered like he was going to whistle. "Focus on slowing your breath."

I tried to do as he said, but my lips trembled too hard to cooperate. Tears filled my eyes, and I closed them again as everything began to go dark around the edges.

"Lauryn, look at me. Focus. Keep your eyes on me. I want you to hold your breath, and I'm going to count to five, and then you can release it. One—"

"I don't want to die," I whispered, unaware I'd actually voiced the thought until he responded.

"You're not gonna die."

"You don't know that!" My voice cracked with fear, and I gulped in an attempt to swallow it down.

"I won't let that happen."

My vision blurred with tears. "Oh, like you have any control over it. You obviously don't read romance novels, because any time the hero tells the heroine he won't let anything happen to her, that's a sure sign that something's going to happen to her."

He lifted an eyebrow and grinned, and I was painfully aware that it might be the last time I ever saw him smile.

"You're right," he said. "I don't read romance novels. And I'm not anyone's hero."

Realizing that I'd basically declared us a couple, I stammered to correct myself. "I wasn't saying that you, well, that we were, I mean, I didn't mean to imply that—"

The plane shuddered again, wobbling from side to side, and I screamed. A huge tear escaped, rolling across my cheek before falling to splash on to the top of my foot.

"Hey," Brick whispered, reaching to wipe away the wetness on my cheek with his thumb. "Listen to me! We're gonna make it, okay? I'm not dying today, and neither are you. I've got more lives than an alley cat, and you wouldn't believe what all I've survived. Now, I made a commitment to get Kirby back to face the court, and I don't go back on a promise once I make it. I'm promising you I will do everything in my power to ensure you make it out of this safely."

The plane shuddered again, the constant vibration growing in intensity. Then with a sudden sharp dip to the left, the plane detonated like a bomb, and hell consumed us in a deafening explosion that seemed to rip us from the sky and propel us into another dimension.

The air around me turned to fire, and we spun so violently I couldn't tell if we were moving up or down, backward or forward. The force against my body reminded me of a ride I'd been on at a carnival as a teen, but rather than the exhilarating thrill of weightlessness and speed, this felt as though at any moment my flesh would simply give way and my bones would be torn apart. My mind shut down in dizzy, desperate self-defense, and just before my world went black, the sky was everywhere, a pinkish-purple blue smeared with streaks of gray.

The last thing to penetrate my consciousness before the unknowing bliss of a dark void swallowed me was a strong arm wrapping around my shoulders and a muscular body covering mine, surrounding me with strength as the world blew apart.

THREE

The realization that the weight on my back was likely Brick's body brought me back into the present moment, and I pushed up with every ounce of strength I could muster. He slumped off me toward his seat, and with the release of his weight, the compression restricting my air intake eased.

I sucked in as much air as I could to fill my desperate lungs as I looked to Brick. He lay crumpled to one side, his body bent at an odd angle, his eyes closed and his jaw slack.

Was he dead? Oh, God. He couldn't be dead.

"Brick?" I called out to him, but he didn't answer.

Kirby groaned behind me, and I turned, my eyes widening in disbelief as I took in my surroundings.

The window Kirby leaned against was still intact, but the wall above it had been torn away to reveal the night sky where the ceiling and overhead bins should have been.

A huge tree had fallen across the back of the plane, its scarred and jagged trunk crushing the seats across the aisle from us and most of the row in front of us. It had missed me by mere inches, and I shuddered to think of how many different ways I'd come close to death in the midst of the crash.

The realization that the passengers in those seats hadn't been so lucky struck me, and my stomach roiled.

Certain I must be in the throes of a nightmare too horrific to comprehend, I pinched my leg as hard as I could, refusing to believe I was awake even as I winced from the self-inflicted pain and the over-powering smell of burnt chemicals filled my nostrils.

I looked down at my hands, my fingers spread wide as I turned my wrists in bewildered confusion, and then I tentatively lifted each foot, bracing for any onslaught of pain, but instead, feeling only a detached numbness.

How on earth was it possible I'd escaped unscathed? How was I not only alive, but seemingly uninjured? If I wasn't sleeping, the only other explanation was Brick.

Brick had placed his body over mine.

Crying out his name again, I reached to shake his shoulder, jerking my hand back as his head lolled forward. Blood covered the back of his head and neck; his black T-shirt glistened with it. My already queasy stomach roiled again as I looked down at the bright red liquid coating my fingertips, and I screamed as I frantically tried to wipe it away on my dress.

"We gotta get outta here," Kirby said next to me, and I jumped as his voice reinforced reality. "It's gonna blow."

"What?" I stared at him, unable to comprehend that even though I'd survived the crash, I wasn't out of danger.

"Don't you smell the smoke? Don't you hear that sizzling?" he asked as he stepped onto his seat to look around. "It's gonna blow. For sure."

Until he'd asked, I hadn't noticed the smoke stinging my eyes and burning my throat, nor had I considered the source of the crackling sound and the intermittent pops. I'd been too overwhelmed to focus, but with the realization the plane was still burning, fear spurred me into action, and I unfastened my seat belt and tried to stand.

My legs buckled the moment I looked forward. In front of the fallen tree, there were at least two more rows where there should have been seats filled with passengers on either side of an aisle. Instead, it was a charred and unrecognizable wasteland that still smoldered in spots. Beyond that was nothing but forest with shattered trees and broken limbs.

"Where's the rest of the plane? Where are the other passengers? The crew?"

"Probably dead," Kirby said, his tone entirely too casual and matter-of-fact. "I think we're the sole survivors, or at least we will be if we can get out of this death trap." He hoisted himself up onto the wall, howling in pain as a piece of torn metal ripped into his palm. "Be careful. There's lots of sharp shit up here."

I frowned at the height of the wall and the jagged fragments jutting out at the top of it. There was no way I could lift myself up and over that. "Isn't there some easier way out?"

"Yeah, if you're wanting to crawl over a bunch of crispy dead people."

I shuddered in revulsion at the reality of his statement and his blasé attitude toward it.

"You coming or not?" he asked.

"What about Brick?"

Kirby glared at me as his balance wobbled atop what was left of the wall. "What about him?"

"We can't just leave him here."

"If he ain't dead yet, he will be soon."

I pressed my fingers into Brick's wrist, praying for a strong pulse that would leave no doubt he was alive.

A steady thump answered my prayers, and I breathed a sigh of relief.

"He's alive," I said to Kirby. "We have to get him out."

Kirby swore as he searched the ground as though he were looking for a safe place to jump. Then he looked back at me with a frown.

"How you think we gonna lift his big ass over this wall? If he was conscious and could help, maybe, but he ain't nothing but dead weight. In more than one way. With all that blood, his head's gotta be messed up bad. Probably took a hit from that tree when it fell. Face it. He's a goner. We need to find the rest of the plane and see if anyone else survived. Maybe they already called for help."

He extended his hand to pull me up, and I shook my head.

"I wouldn't be here if it wasn't for Brick. He got me out of the way of that cart and into a seat, and somehow, he protected me when things went to hell. I'm not leaving him here to die."

Kirby shrugged, pulling his hand back. "Yeah, well, I wouldn't be here if it wasn't for him either, and I ain't about to risk my life to save the guy just so he can haul me back to jail. I'm telling you, this thing is gonna blow. If you don't get out now, you're gonna blow with it."

"But he's alive! He's breathing! We can't just leave him here."

Kirby clucked his tongue against his teeth and swore. "Suit yourself. You're on your own. I ain't going out that way. I didn't survive coming down just to go back up in bits and pieces."

He jumped down, and I turned my attention back to Brick.

"You gotta wake up, big guy." I squeezed his hand and then patted his cheek firmly, but he didn't respond to either. "Kirby's right on both counts. Something may blow up or catch fire again, so we need to get out of here, but I can't lift you over that wall."

Running my fingers over his scalp, I located a gash on the back of his head and another just behind his ear. Neither seemed to be very deep, but both were seeping blood, and I knew I had to do something to stop the flow. But first, I had to get him some place safer, and to do that, I had to find a way out.

The tree filled the aisle, but even if it hadn't, going forward through the burned area wasn't an option, especially since it would be impossible for me to drag Brick through it.

I stood and looked back toward the galley. There hadn't been an exit route there before, but it also hadn't had a tree laying on top of it, and it had a ceiling then, so anything was possible.

Stepping onto my seat and over Brick's legs, I climbed onto the huge tree trunk, bracing myself in case it shifted or dropped beneath me. It held, and I crawled along past the smashed partition wall between the galley and the seats across the aisle from us.

The impact of the tail section hitting the tree had torn apart the outer galley wall on the other side, leaving an opening beneath the tree that looked wide enough for me to squeeze through. But how would I get Brick from his seat to the opening? No way could I heft him up on the tree.

Jumping down from the trunk inside the galley, I knelt to look beneath it. There might be enough clearance to pull him under the tree, but even if there was, how would I get his broad shoulders through the narrow opening in the outer wall?

Unfortunately, I had little time to find other options. Already, the black smoke was thicker, making it harder to breathe. The bitter chemical smell that permeated my nostrils with each inhale left no doubt that it was toxic. As if the threat of being blown to smithereens at any second wasn't enough, I now had to worry that one or both of us might die from asphyxiation.

I rushed back to Brick, pausing to grab some paper towels from the lavatory to use for makeshift bandages. After layering them together and folding them, I pressed the thick strips against his gashes and then looked around for something to hold them into place. The curtain hanging between his seat and the galley entrance was pulled back with a sash, and I ripped it from the wall and wrapped it around his head, pulling one end through the metal grommet on the other end to secure it.

Positioning myself with one leg on either side of his thigh, I bent and put my arms beneath his shoulders and pulled, but even with my most valiant effort, I could only lift him a few inches. Panic set in as the black smoke billowed around us, burning my eyes, nose, and throat. If I couldn't figure out a way to get us out into fresh air soon, we'd both be overcome and suffocate.

I tried again to lift him, but the strain triggered a coughing spell that left me dizzy.

Time was running out. Neither of us could survive much longer.

Shifting my feet to the narrow opening between Brick's seat and the tree trunk, I changed my strategy, leveraging my back against the tree to pull him sideways. After much effort and more than a few pleas heavenward, I managed to finagle him out of his seat, but as I shuffled my feet toward the galley, his weight shifted, pinning me beneath him with my back against the tree and our bodies wedged between the trunk and the galley wall.

A high-pitched whizzing sound rang out through the air, followed by a series of pops, and the terror-driven adrenaline coursing through my veins was like an electrical current on the verge of short-circuiting. My pulse pounded inside my head, each beat ticking like a countdown clock on a bomb rigged to blow at any moment.

For the second time in one day, my own death seemed imminent, but I refused to give up. With a roar of desperation and a determination to survive, I shoved upward with everything I had. Brick's body lifted just enough that I could slide toward the galley, ignoring the fiery sensation of the bark scraping my back through the thin fabric of my dress.

Once I'd cleared the galley wall, gravity took over, and Brick fell to the floor with a heavy thud and a pained grunt, though he remained unconscious.

"Sorry about that, big guy," I mumbled as I adjusted the sash around his head. Then, I grabbed his ankles and began to crawl backward beneath the tree. I cracked my head against its underside, but I didn't even flinch. I just kept moving with a laser focus, pulling Brick with me.

It took some maneuvering for me to get through the jagged opening in the outer wall, and even more effort to get Brick through, but somehow, I got us both outside the plane.

My lungs burned as though they were on fire. My throat was beyond raw, and my eyes stung so badly my vision blurred. I was dizzy from the chemical smells, the lack of oxygen, and the bump on my head. My arms and legs trembled with the exertion of pulling Brick's weight and lifting him.

But I had no time to rest or recover because we weren't out of danger yet.

I moved to put my arms beneath his shoulders and continued dragging him across the ground. He groaned loudly a few times during the journey, and though I was certain it meant I was causing him pain, I didn't dare stop until we were far enough away to be safe from the contaminated air and the threat of fire or explosion.

When I finally reached an area where the air seemed clear, I released Brick and then doubled over in a violent coughing fit.

Once I caught my breath, I lifted my eyes to look back at the fuselage. The entire scene looked more like a movie set than anything that could be real. The tail fin sat upright, seemingly unscathed as it towered above the fallen tree. The hole on this side of the plane was larger than I'd realized before, and from this new vantage point, I could see that a portion of the seats on this side must have been lost prior to hitting the ground. The magnitude of the death laid out before me was inescapable when viewed from farther away, and my stomach seemed to cave in on itself as I processed what I was seeing. What I had survived. What so many others had not.

Brick moaned, and I knelt beside him.

"Can you hear me?" I whispered, but only a croak of sound came out. "Brick?"

He didn't respond, and I pressed my fingers beneath his jaw, relieved to find he still had a steady pulse.

I checked his paper towel bandages and tightened the sash as best I could, and then I rolled him onto his side into the recovery position and adjusted his head to ensure he had good airflow. It seemed a moot point to take such ordinary precautions after I'd pulled him over a seat and under a tree and then jostled him across the rough forest floor, but I was determined to do all I could.

When I was satisfied that his breathing was normal, I collapsed onto my back on the ground beside him. Hot tears streamed from my eyes, as much from the smoke as from emotion. I had a terrible stitch in my side and a painful throbbing in my head. My arms and legs ached, and my skin was scraped and torn and bruised in too many places to count, but none of that hurt as much as my lungs. No matter how deeply I tried to breathe, it didn't feel as though I was getting any air.

Everything began to go black around the edges again, and I didn't have the energy to fight it. I closed my eyes and let the darkness take me.

FOUR

When I woke, the sky above me was clear, filled with the twinkling lights of infinite stars against a background so dark it was void of any color.

The ground beneath me was cold, and my body ached all over. My throat and mouth were so parched the insides of my cheeks stuck to my teeth and I couldn't muster enough saliva to swallow.

I remembered seeing a water bottle laying on the floor of the galley next to the overturned beverage cart, and the thought of the cool liquid soothing my throat drove me to sit up. I moved slowly, but my head still swam with the effort.

Looking toward the wreckage, I was relieved to see the galley section still intact. Smoke still rose in wisps but no longer billowed, and there were no visible flames.

Brick remained in the position I had put him in, and I worried I might find his skin cold and unyielding with death as I reached to check for a pulse. It took me a moment to find it, and I frowned at how much weaker it was than before.

Pushing myself to stand on shaky legs, I tried to take in a deep breath, but my lungs could only expand so far before I'd end up coughing. My throat burned like I'd swallowed hot coals, and I struggled to swallow as I stumbled toward the fuselage, desperate for water.

An eerie quiet filled the air, as though the frogs and crickets had fallen silent, waiting in anticipation for what might happen next.

Thick forest surrounded me on all sides, the trees so densely packed it was impossible to see beyond the first few feet. The light from the sky cast a dim illumination on the clearing created by the tail section's arrival, but it was unable to penetrate the depths of the woods. I stared into the darkness and wondered if anything out there was staring back at me.

I shivered at the thought as a cool night breeze brushed across my bare arms and legs, and when I moved to hug my torso, I felt the small backpack strapped to my chest.

I'd been so focused on the imminent danger before that I hadn't even realized I still wore it. I tore it open with a gasp and pulled out my cell phone, praying for a signal as I powered it back on.

The phone lit up with a screensaver photo of me and my cousins Dani and Piper in a laughing group hug, and a longing for home hit me so intensely that it felt like a punch in my gut.

I thought of my mother, who had expected to pick me up this evening. I had no concept of how long it would take for someone to realize we'd fallen from the sky and notify our families. Had she driven to the airport without knowing I wouldn't arrive? Had she been alone when they told her? Perhaps they'd reached her before she left home. Then at least she would have had my dad or my brother with her. Maybe even an aunt or uncle, a cousin or two. I pictured my family gathered together, distraught as they waited for news, and a pain seized my chest. I needed to reach them. To let them know I was alive. That they didn't need to worry or grieve for me.

The word *Searching* appeared at the top of the phone's screen where the carrier name should be, and I shook it gently as though that might encourage it.

"C'mon, c'mon," I murmured as I waited, but then the status changed to *No Signal*, crushing any hope I'd held. "No, no, no. Please, no."

I began to cough again as emotions overwhelmed me, and my need for water became paramount. Shoving the phone back in my bag, I continued toward the wreckage but as I got closer, I stopped in my tracks.

While I'd certainly been aware of the bodies surrounding me earlier, the smoke had blanketed them in a haze, and I'd been consumed by the urgent need to escape and survive. Now with the smoke mostly cleared and my mind less distracted, it was impossible not to see the passenger remains. My stomach revolted at the gruesome scene, but my heart took it the hardest. These were wives, husbands, daughters, sons, mothers, fathers, cousins, and friends. So many souls gone in a matter of minutes. So many lives cut tragically short.

I couldn't bear to think of their families and what they'd lost, of the news they'd soon be receiving.

How on earth was it fair that I'd survived when they hadn't? Why had some odd twist of fate put me in the one row that sat unharmed? Why me?

It would have been easy to spiral down that emotional rabbit hole, but I knew I couldn't allow myself to do that yet. So, with an odd mixture of guilt and relief twisting in my gut, I forced myself to turn away from the reality of the dead and focus on staying alive.

First, I needed water. Then, I had to figure out a way to get help for Brick and get us both out of this situation.

But with no cell signal and no way to get him off the mountain, what more could I do?

I wondered if Kirby had found the rest of the plane and if there had been other survivors. There had to be. We three couldn't be the only ones. I needed to believe there were others.

Perhaps someone had already called for help and a rescue mission was under way. Even if they hadn't, the pilots had known before the crash that we were in trouble. Undoubtedly, they had given the plane's location to someone on the other end of the radio. With that to go on, it should only be a matter of time before rescuers came, but it worried me that our piece of the plane wasn't with the rest.

I assumed any tracking technology would be located with the cockpit, so that would be where rescuers would go. *How far away from them were we? And how would they know where to find us? Was the path of destruction caused by our spinning tail section enough to make it visible from the air?*

If Kirby was with the others, he should be able to lead them back to us, but as I considered his parting words and his animosity toward Brick, I couldn't be so sure he would. He might retaliate against his captor by leaving us stranded. I had no way of knowing what he might be capable of, but Brick obviously didn't trust him. Of course, I didn't know Brick either.

As I bent to look through the opening that led to the galley, my body froze in revolt against going back in. It had to be done; I knew that. But the necessity of it didn't stop my heart from pounding or keep my stomach from flipping. I could think of a long list of places I'd rather be than inside that dark, claustrophobic, toxic, death-ridden, steel graveyard, but since wishing couldn't transport me away, I squared my shoulders and knelt to go under the tree, determined to get it over with as quickly as possible.

It seemed much darker than before, despite the lack of smoke filling the air. My imagination went into overdrive as I crawled low to the ground beneath the tree, my fingers stretched ahead of me to feel my way along. I was keenly aware of the numerous dead bodies mere feet away from me, and though I knew it wasn't likely anyone had ended up in the galley, I still feared I'd make contact with dead flesh each time I moved forward.

My skin crawled as I shuddered in fear, but then it dawned on me that I had my phone in my bag and could use its flashlight feature.

I reached in to draw it out but then hesitated. *Did I really want to see what horrors might be keeping me company? Would it be better not to know?*

After weighing what I might see against what I might unknowingly touch, I opted to be aware and informed. I pulled the phone out and put its light on the dimmest setting, wanting to preserve as much battery life as I could.

My resolve to know what might be there didn't prevent me from cringing as I swept the light around the confined space, wary of what its beam may reveal. Once I'd determined that I was indeed alone, I scrambled under the tree and over to the beverage cart lying on its side in the galley.

Grabbing a bottle of water, I tossed the cap aside and turned it up, but the sudden rush of liquid felt like salt in an open wound as it went down my throat, setting off yet another coughing fit. Once that subsided, I sipped the water more slowly, savoring its cool comfort.

With a nervous glance over my shoulder toward the cabin and the horrors it held, I gathered up the remaining bottles of water, juice, and soda and tossed them under the tree toward the opening in the outer wall. Then, I shoved packets of cookies and pretzels into my backpack and down the front of my bra. Next, I pulled open any cabinets or drawers that were still operational, which yielded a first aid kit, two paltry pillows, and a couple of thin blankets.

I had just climbed through the opening and stepped outside after tossing everything onto the ground when a voice rang out in the darkness.

"You're still alive, eh?"

FIVE

Completely caught off-guard and already on edge, I screamed and tried to retreat, but my back was against the plane.

"Whoa, hold up, there, girl!" Kirby said as he walked toward me with both hands raised. "It's just me. I didn't mean to scare you."

I bent to brace my hands on my knees as another fit of violent coughs racked my body.

"You okay?" he asked.

All the water I'd consumed was on its way back up, and I had just enough time to step away from the items I'd gathered before it spewed forth.

Kirby turned his back to me, and once my retching was done, I stood and wiped my mouth with the back of my hand.

"Sorry," I said in a croak. "Hope I didn't get anything on you."

He mumbled something, and then covered his mouth. Then he bent to dry heave a couple of times before looking toward the sky with a stream of curse words.

"I don't do well with people getting sick," he said once he'd composed himself, though he still looked a little queasy.

It struck me as ironic that he had been so cavalier regarding death and the presence of charred and mangled bodies, yet the sight of someone throwing up water did him in.

"Did you find the rest of the plane?" I asked.

He frowned as he nodded, and my heart sank.

"Did anyone else...make it?"

His frown deepened and he shook his head. "It's at the bottom of a canyon not far from here. There ain't nothing left but ashes. It musta been a fireball even before it hit the mountain."

Tears sprang to my eyes and my knees went weak. All those people. All those lives. So much heartache. And then even as I felt guilty for thinking it, my mind began to race, wondering what that meant for us. For our rescue.

"Will they still be able to find us? Will they know we're out here? That we got separated?"

"Beats me," Kirby said with a shrug.

"They'll probably find the larger crash site first, won't they? Maybe we should try to get Brick there so he can get help quicker."

Kirby's eyebrows shot up and his eyes widened. "He's still alive?"

"Yeah. He was when I left him a few minutes ago. I came to get supplies. You want a water?"

I bent and picked up a bottle to hand to him, and he snatched it from me and guzzled it down like a man who'd been wandering the desert.

He'd torn a sleeve from his T-shirt and wrapped it around his injured hand. The blood had soaked through, dripping down his arm in trickles of red as he held the water bottle up.

After finishing the first one, he picked up a second and downed it.

"Hey," I cautioned. "We might want to take it slow. I don't know how long it will be before we get rescued, and there's not a lot of water. They'd almost finished the beverage service, so it wasn't a full cart."

He ignored my pleas and continued to chug until the second

bottle was empty. Then he picked up a pack of cookies I'd dropped and tore it open, shoving them into his mouth.

"Yeah, well, I ain't sticking around," he said around the cookies, crumbs flying from his mouth. "They'll rescue you but arrest me."

The hairs on my arms and along the back of my neck bristled with the reminder that Kirby was likely dangerous.

"What did you do?" The words popped out of my mouth before I could stop them.

"Nothing," he said, swallowing the last of the cookies as he tossed the empty bag on the ground. "But they're gonna send me back to jail anyway."

He squatted near the pile of supplies and began shoving waters and cookies into his pockets and inside the waistband of his jeans.

"Wait, what are you doing?" I rushed forward, tossing aside the possibility that he might be dangerous in my quest to preserve supplies. "We have to share that. We need to ration it for the three of us and make it last."

"I told you I ain't sticking around."

"Where on earth are you going to go? We're in the middle of nowhere."

"Maybe. Maybe not. There's a canyon not too far from here, and I see lights on the other side. Figure maybe it's a house, and I could find a phone, or at least a place to get some sleep. Then once the sun's up, I'll find a road and head toward a town. You should come with me."

The mere thought of wandering into those dense, black woods sent chills up my spine, and I shuddered and hugged my arms around me. I wouldn't even be willing to venture into that darkness with someone I trusted implicitly, much less a stranger I knew to be a criminal. It was such an alarming concept that I was willing to try and talk Kirby into staying, even though he made me uncomfortable.

"You sure you don't want to wait until morning? Until daylight? I don't think it's safe to be out there in the dark."

Kirby's scoffing laugh seemed harsh and loud in the eerie quiet of the night as he unzipped the first aid kit and dug out a bandage for his hand. "You think it's safe sitting here? The bears and coyotes might have run away from the crash, but as soon as they get a whiff of those corpses, they'll be back. And they'd prefer a live one like you over one squished under a tree or burnt to a crisp any day."

His irreverent reference to the dead repulsed me, but his valid point about wildlife shook me. I looked toward the woods again, even more wary about what might be watching me from the dark depths.

Once he'd finished bandaging his hand, he stood with over half the supplies I'd gathered tucked into his clothing. "You coming or not?"

"I already told you; I'm not leaving Brick."

"If he ain't awake by now, he ain't gonna make it."

I glanced back toward where Brick lay just past the edge of the woods.

"He'll make it," I said, lifting my chin in defiance. He had to. I'd worked too hard to get Brick out for him to die on me now.

Kirby grinned. "I don't get why you're so worked up over somebody you don't even know. You really got the hots for him, don't ya?"

"What? Don't be ridiculous," I protested, though I knew there was more truth in his words than I cared to admit. "I'm not worked up. I just want to see a fellow human being survive, okay?"

"Right. Okay. Whatever you say. I saw the two of you making eyes at each other back at the airport and on the plane before it all went to shit. But let me give you a heads up on this one. That guy—he don't do romance or girlfriends or whatever. He's about as much of a loner as they come."

"Wait, you know him? I thought—"

"I know what you thought. And yeah, he was bringing me back to Florida to face a judge. But I've known Brick since I was a kid, and I'm telling you, you're wasting your time with that one. Even if he does survive."

Kirby turned to go, and I resisted the urge to stop him and ask him more questions about Brick. It was none of my business, after all, and it wasn't like it mattered. When Brick regained consciousness—I refused to think in terms of *if*—we'd get rescued and go our separate ways.

Kirby disappeared into the trees, and the night seemed even quieter and more ominous. I missed the company, even if I didn't care for his.

Gathering the supplies he'd left behind, I juggled as much as I could carry over to where Brick lay. He hadn't moved at all, and when I reached to check his pulse, his skin felt colder than before.

Was it just the night air, or had the loss of blood slowed his circulation too much to keep him warm?

Helplessness formed a huge lump in my throat, and I couldn't swallow it down. I desperately wanted him to live, but I didn't know what else to do to save him.

I wished I could call my mother. She'd know what to do. In addition to knowledge gained from a lifetime of nursing, Mom had an iron stomach, unflappable courage, and a never-ending supply of calm. She'd tried to teach my brother and me as much as she could about first aid, but I'd always taken for granted that she was a phone call away and would be able to direct me if I needed guidance.

Now, here I was, all alone with a man's life in my hands, and I would have given anything to be able to call my mom and ask her what to do.

Pulling my phone out of my purse, I powered it up again with a wish and prayer, but when it still said *No Signal*, I reluctantly turned it back off to conserve the battery.

"*Keep it together, Lauryn,*" I said to myself, hearing Mom's voice clearly in my head. "*Just stay calm, and do what you can, the best you can.*"

Nodding to the mental image of her, I blew out a loud exhale and went to work.

I unfolded the blanket Kirby had left behind and laid it over Brick, tucking it in around him. It was only a lap blanket, too small to cover his huge frame, but I hoped the added layer would help shield him against the chilly night air.

Then, I opened the first aid kit and rummaged through it, relieved to see Kirby had left behind the antiseptic ointment and butterfly bandages. Setting aside the blood-soaked paper towels and sash, I used the wet wipes to clean Brick's skin as best I could before applying the ointment and fresh bandages. His thick, wavy hair made it nearly impossible to get the adhesive to stick, but without a razor to clear the area, there was little else I could do.

When I'd finished, I knelt beside him, willing him to make it. Lying perfectly still with his eyes closed, he looked like a Greek statue. I felt the strangest attachment to him, far stronger than what made sense for a man I didn't even know. I reasoned that it was likely due to our situation and what we'd been through together, even though he was unconscious. He had given me focus, distraction, and purpose in the midst of a terrifying experience, so it made since that I would feel bonded to him. Of course, I also didn't want to be left alone on the top of the mountain with yet another corpse for company, so that factored into my determination for his survival as well.

But something had existed between us even before the flight went haywire. From the first moment I saw Brick, I felt the oddest sensation of belonging. Something deep within me had stirred, and I wanted to know what that was, what it meant.

He had to survive. He had to wake up. He had to look at me again with those brilliant blue eyes. I refused to believe that a connection so powerful was destined to end before it even began.

Leaning forward, I cupped his cheek in my hand, the stubble of his jaw rough against my palm. I longed to press my lips against his, hoping for some Sleeping Beauty moment where the prince would awaken from true love's kiss and we'd get off the damned mountain and live happily ever after.

But this wasn't a fairy tale. This was an unconscious man who had no way of consenting to being kissed, and though it was highly unlikely he'd ever know it had happened, I would know, and I'd be ashamed of my disrespect. I certainly wouldn't want some stranger kissing me if I was incapable of agreeing to it.

"Hi, Brick," I whispered, opting for a polite plea instead. "It's Lauryn, the girl from the plane. It was, um, nice to meet you, but we didn't really get a chance to talk. Why don't you wake up and tell me more about yourself? So far, you haven't exactly been the life of the party, but I'm willing to give you another chance, considering the circumstances. Besides, I could really use some help figuring out what to do next. Disaster stories aren't really my thing, but I'm holding out hope for a happy ending."

"This is insanity," I told myself as I turned to clean up the bandage wrappers and soiled paper towels and wipes. *"I'm literally having a one-way conversation with an unconscious stranger. This is how the break from reality begins. And now I'm talking to myself, which is likely another sign that I'm losing it. God, I need sleep. I need something to eat other than cookies."*

After scrubbing my fingers and palms with another wipe and a couple of drops of hand sanitizer from my bag, I rubbed my hands up and down my arms, trying to generate warmth. The ground had grown even colder along with the night air, and I first cursed myself for wearing a thin sundress and sandals for the flight, and then I cursed Kirby for taking the other blanket.

Brick moaned and shifted his weight slightly, his first movement since I'd carried him from the plane.

Rushing to kneel at his side, I laid my hands on either side of his face, patting his cheeks lightly. "Brick? Brick, can you hear me? Please wake up!"

He didn't respond to my pleas, but his body trembled, and then he huddled beneath the blanket and reached to pull it tighter. It was the most he'd moved since the crash, and hope sprang within me.

He might not be conscious yet, but he was still there. Still hanging on. And he was cold, which meant there might be something more I could do after all. Something that would help us both.

SIX

"Okay, big guy," I said as I grabbed the thin paper-covered airline pillow and stretched out behind him on the ground. "I want to make it clear that I am doing this for warmth and survival, okay? Please do not get the wrong impression."

I lifted the edge of the blanket and wriggled beneath it. It wasn't nearly wide enough to cover us both, but I hoped our combined heat beneath it would be enough to warm him. I positioned my body alongside his, trying to ignore the sensations caused by the soft fleshiness of my breasts pressed against the rigid firmness of his muscular back.

Though his face and neck were cool to the touch above the blanket, his torso was considerably warmer. Relieved, I moved even closer against him, tucking my knees behind his as I sought the same relief from the cold that I offered him.

At first, I held myself rigid, uncomfortably aware that I was nestled against a stranger. But the longer I lay there, the harder it was to stay tense. The ground was cold and hard, and our circumstances were still dire, but something about human contact made me feel less alone, and the state of extreme anxiety I'd been in for the last couple of hours began to ease its grip.

A weary exhaustion set in, and my eyelids grew heavy as I leaned into Brick's solidness even more.

I hadn't intended to fall asleep, and I would have thought it impossible with the threat of the unknown in the woods, the worry over Brick's health and our rescue, and the ever-decreasing temperatures.

But the next thing I knew, I was having the most wonderful dream. I was still snuggled against Brick, but in the dream, we had rolled over together to spoon in the opposite direction with his strong arm encircling my waist and his nose nuzzled into the curve of my neck. Instinctively, I moved my hips back against his, sliding my hand over his forearm as I marveled at the strength of the corded muscles beneath my fingers. He responded by tucking his legs in tighter behind mine, pulling me closer in his embrace as his lips trailed across my skin.

I turned my face toward his, eager to feel his kiss, but then I made the mistake of opening my eyes.

The warm, lush bed of my dreams disappeared, and I jerked away from Brick's embrace and jumped to my feet, horrified at my wanton behavior while asleep.

His eyes blinked open with a startled expression as he tried to sit up, but then his hands went to his head and his face contorted into a pained grimace.

"What the hell?" His voice was thick and hoarse.

"Hold on, hold on!" I said, kneeling to take his hands and move them gently away from his bandages. "You can't touch those."

He slumped backward, and I wrapped my arms around his shoulders, helping him to lie back down.

"Slow down there, big guy. You gotta take it easy."

Grabbing the tiny pillow to place it beneath his head, I looked down at him as he stared up at me, his brows furrowed, and I could practically see the wheels turning inside his head as he tried to process what was happening.

"Where...what..." He closed his eyes and lifted his hand to his head again.

Taking his hand in mine, I pulled it away to lay it on his chest.

"You have a couple of pretty nasty gashes, and what I think is a bad concussion. At least I hope that's all it is. You've been out for a few hours."

His eyes opened, narrowing them as he considered my words, and his brows furrowed tighter in confusion.

"How...where...what happened?"

"Our plane crashed. I don't know if you remember me, but I'm Lauryn. We met briefly before we went down. Somehow, me, you, and Kirby are the only three who survived."

His eyes widened, and he tried to sit up again. He swayed to one side and I reached to catch him, but he dodged my effort as he planted his palm on the ground to steady himself.

"Dude, you gotta go slowly. Did you not hear me say you have a head injury?"

"Where's Kirby?" he asked, his voice gruff.

"He went to try and find a house."

Rolling to shift his weight onto his knees, he lifted his head to survey the wreckage.

"Damn. Where's the rest of the plane?"

"I don't know. Kirby said he found it and that there wasn't anything left. We're the only survivors." A chill ran up my spine as I said the awful truth aloud. "I can't believe it. What are the chances?"

"He left and came back?" Brick pushed himself to stand, holding his hands out to steady himself.

"Yeah. He came back and took a whole bunch of stuff I'd gotten from the plane. Said he'd seen a light across a canyon, and he was gonna head for it to see if he could make a call or crash for the night." I cringed as I realized what I'd said. "Sorry. Bad choice of words. He said he'd try to find a road into town in the morning."

Brick stumbled forward a few steps and then reeled, slamming his shoulder into a tree.

"I don't think you should push yourself," I said, rushing to his side in case he fell, though there's no way I could have caught him. "You might have a bad concussion, and at the very least, you're likely to be dizzy. Maybe just take it easy."

He squeezed his eyes shut as he rested his forehead against the tree trunk, his face scrunched with pain. "How long ago did he leave?"

"I don't know. Maybe a couple of hours ago?" I pulled my phone from my purse and turned it on to check the time. "I don't have a signal, but the clock still seems to work, and I had the phone on fairly soon after Kirby left. So yeah, he's been gone a couple of hours."

He pulled his own phone from his pocket and frowned.

"My battery's dead. Can I see that?" He reached for my phone, and I handed it to him. He frowned again as he looked at it, and then he held it up toward the sky. "No signal up this high. There's probably not a cell tower anywhere close."

I powered the phone off when he returned it and then put it back in my bag.

"You said you salvaged items from the plane?" he asked, squinting with one eye.

"Yeah!" I moved to my pile of goodies and grabbed a water. "You should probably drink something."

He took the bottle and began to chug the water with much the same intensity as Kirby had.

I was so relieved to see him awake and talking that I wanted to rush over and hug him, but I had to remind myself that he had no idea what all we'd been through together and might be taken aback at such familiarity.

"What?" he asked, wiping his hand across his mouth once he'd finished the water. "What's so funny?"

"Nothing." My cheeks flushed hot with embarrassment. I'd been standing there gawking at him with a huge grin on my face. "I'm...

I'm just happy to see you up and about, that's all. I didn't think you were gonna make it there for a while. You were out cold for a long time."

"Was Kirby injured?"

"He cut his hand climbing out of the plane, but other than that, he seemed fine."

"Which direction did he go?"

I pointed toward the last place I'd seen Kirby, and Brick peered into the darkness for a moment before turning back to the fuselage.

"Was there anything else salvageable?"

"I don't know," I said with a shrug. "I went back in specifically for water and food. We have cookies and pretzels if you're hungry."

He began walking toward the plane, and I followed behind him, ignoring the feeling of dread at the prospect of seeing those bodies again.

"Damn," he whispered under his breath as we got closer. "We survived that, huh?"

"Crazy, isn't it?"

He stopped and turned back to me, then he looked beyond me to where we'd been lying on the ground. His brow furrowed close again and the confused look returned. "How did we get all the way over there?"

"I dragged you."

His eyebrows lifted as his eyes opened wide. "You *dragged* me?"

"Well, yeah." My words tumbled out in a rush as I tried to explain everything all at once. "I know I probably shouldn't have moved you since you were injured, but before he left, Kirby said the whole thing might blow, and even if it didn't, it was still smoldering, so there was the fire to worry about it, and I know the air seems clear now, but before it was thick and black, and I'm fairly certain it was toxic, so I couldn't leave you where you were, and I couldn't carry you, obviously, so I dragged you, which, yes, in hindsight, probably resulted in you suffering a few extra bumps and bruises, but at the time, I didn't know what else to do."

He stared at me as though I'd grown an extra head. "Are you insane?"

Indignation rose in my throat. *After all I'd gone through to save him, that was his reaction?*

"I think the words you're looking for are *thank you.*"

"I'm sorry. Yes, thank you, obviously, but why would you take that kind of risk for me?"

I shrugged. "Because you're a human being? I couldn't just leave you to die. Especially after you...well, you protected me and you probably saved my life, so I figured I owed you one."

I refrained from mentioning that it was also because I'd hoped to someday marry him and have his babies. I figured that might be too much too soon.

He closed his mouth and glanced back at the wreckage before taking a long look at me.

"Thanks. Really. I'm...I don't even know what to say." Cocking his head to the side, he looked at me even more intently, as though seeing me for the first time. "Are you all right? Were you injured?"

"No." I shook my head. "Thanks to you and whatever bizarre twist of fate decided to leave our row intact. That tree missed us by inches. Well, it missed me and Kirby. I think it might be what cracked you in the head, but I don't know for sure."

He laid one hand on the tree trunk and reached up to touch his injuries with the other.

"You did this? The bandages?"

"Be careful; they didn't stick very well with your hair in the way, but I didn't have any way to shave it. I don't know how long they'll stay on. We have a few more if we need to change them out."

"Where'd you find bandages?"

"There was a first aid kit in one of the cabinets in the galley."

He stared at the tree where it lay across the back of the plane. "You were able to get inside the galley?"

"Yeah. Once you crawl under the tree, you can stand up inside, and most of the galley is still intact."

"So, you already got everything we could use?"

"I don't know if I got *everything*. I raided the beverage cart, and then I opened a few cabinets and drawers, but I'll admit I was more than a little creeped out by being in there, so I might have overlooked something. I was mostly looking for food, water, and something to help stop your bleeding."

He squatted next to the plane to peer into the darkness beyond the hole. "This is how you came in and out?"

"Yeah. If you go around the front, it's...it's..." I struggled to find the words to describe what he'd find, shuddering at the memory of what I had seen and couldn't unsee. "Let's just say the fire pretty much destroyed...everything...in the rows ahead of ours."

Pulling his keys from his front jeans pocket, he clicked the button on the end of a tiny cylinder flashlight, and a dim beam shone inside the galley.

Brick crawled beneath the tree and into the dark fuselage, and my heart began to pound. I don't know if it was the fear of something happening to him, flashbacks of being in that darkness, or the sensation of being alone outside—and perhaps it was all three—but my anxiety level shot through the roof, and once again, I found it hard to breathe. The acrid odor of death and chemicals lingering in the air didn't help matters, and soon another coughing fit racked my body. Try as I might to get it under control, I couldn't stop. Fearing I might pass out again, I leaned against the side of the plane for support.

SEVEN

Brick's face was crinkled with concern as he came crawling back out and stood next to me.

"Are you all right?"

I couldn't stop coughing long enough to respond.

Brick patted my back hard, and when that didn't help, he tried lifting my arm, tugging it high in the air, but it was no use. The coughs were relentless.

"Here," he said, reaching for a bottle of water I'd left on the ground when I'd gathered everything after Kirby left. He unscrewed the cap and held the bottle to my lips, tilting it up as I struggled to swallow.

More water went down the front of my dress than down my throat, but eventually I swallowed enough to relax the muscles and stop coughing.

"You sure you're okay?" he asked as I swiped away tears with my knuckles.

I nodded, though I wasn't at all sure that I was. My lungs burned as badly as they had when I was surrounded by smoke, and my throat was raw again.

"Here, try to drink a little more." He lifted the bottle to my lips again, his frown etching deep lines in his face.

After taking a couple more sips, I motioned toward the plane. "I think it's just the...the air...it doesn't bother you?"

"Oh, it's toxic as hell. Why don't you go back over where we were before, where it's a little easier to breathe?"

Eager to leave the horrific setting behind again, I set out toward the blanket, but the coughing spell had left me lightheaded and unsteady on my feet. I stumbled on the uneven ground, pitching forward.

Without hesitation, Brick swept me up and into his arms as though I were a rag doll.

"What are you doing?" I shrieked, frantically reaching to cover my exposed rump with my hand, though there was no one around to see my panties flashing beneath the short skirt. "Put me down."

As rapidly as he'd picked me up, he put me back down, his frown even deeper. "Sorry. I thought you were fainting or something. Besides, even though I don't read romance novels, I thought it was standard practice for heroes to carry damsels in distress."

"I'm not a damsel in distress, thank you very much. I can walk on my own." To prove the point, I set out toward the blanket. "Besides, I thought you said you weren't anyone's hero."

"I'm not, but I would think by the very definition of the words, you are indeed a damsel in distress." He swept his hand around to indicate our environment. "Are you not?"

My throat hurt too much to argue the point, and I was in no mood to be teased, so I ignored the question and kept walking. When I reached the blanket, I spread it across the ground and plopped down on its edge, drawing the rest of it around me. I opened my tiny backpack and dug around in the bottom, relieved to find three pieces of peppermint.

I popped one in my mouth and began to suck on it, hoping it might ease my throat and my cough, and then I smoothed gloss on my lips to keep them from chapping in the cold.

Brick had disappeared back into the fuselage, and without him next to me, the immense darkness of the woods seemed to swallow me. The black was absolute beneath the trees, and I couldn't see more than a few feet in any direction other than that of the cleared crash site where the moon had space to shine through.

A twig snapped behind me, and I spun so fast my aching head swam. I squinted, straining to see any movement in the darkness as Kirby's warning about bears and coyotes played over and over in my head.

The songs of the night creatures had returned, and I almost missed the eerie silence. At least when the frogs, crickets, and such were quiet, I could hear if anything larger approached.

Raising up on my knees, I began to search the ground around the blanket for any sizable stick. I spotted a branch within reach that appeared to have been snapped off during the crash. It was roughly two feet long, and about as big around as my arm, but it was better than nothing. If a bear or coyote did come ambling out of the darkness toward me, I wouldn't go down without a fight.

I stood and widened my stance, the blanket wrapped around me like a cloak and the branch clutched in my right hand like a sword. My body buzzed with adrenaline, and my head and heart both pounded with the heightened level of fear and the intense strain of watching and listening.

The quiet rustle of footsteps behind me made me whirl, and Brick threw his hands up in surrender as I brandished my stick toward him.

"Damn," he said with raised eyebrows. "What's up?"

He left his hands up even though I'd lowered the stick.

"I heard a noise in the woods." I turned back around, still uneasy about what might be out there watching. "Kirby mentioned there might be bears or coyotes around."

Dropping his hands, Brick stepped past me to look in the same direction. "And you're going to fight them off with a tree branch? I stand corrected. There's no damsel in distress here."

"I might not be able to fight them off, but I figured if I could make myself look more like a threat, it might discourage them from attacking."

"True," he said, looking back at me with his hands on his hips. "Depending on how ornery or hungry they are, of course. Bears are coming out of hibernation this time of year. They might see you as a tasty morsel worth the fight."

His eyes never left mine, but the intensity of his gaze felt like an appraisal, and I got the idea that perhaps he was inclined to agree with the bear.

My cheeks flushed warm, and the jolt of attraction I'd experienced earlier danced across my skin, leaving a ripple of gooseflesh.

"I didn't mean it as an insult, by the way," he said, his voice softening. "The damsel in distress thing."

His eyes seemed to pierce my very soul, and I swallowed hard, questioning my sanity. How on earth could I be feeling a surge of desire in the midst of the tragedy and horror surrounding us?

I tore my gaze from his, determined to break the spell. "Yeah, well, based solely on the definitions, I suppose it's accurate, but I don't like the word *damsel*. It sounds like some weakling standing around wringing her hands waiting for a savior. The phrase has a negative connotation that I don't want to be associated with. I don't need some guy to ride in on a white steed and rescue me. I can take care of myself."

A wry grin lifted the corner of his mouth. "Oh, I have no doubt that you can, but if a guy showed up on a white steed right now, I hope you'd be smart enough to climb on the horse with him and get out of here. I sure as hell would. And I wouldn't give a damn what the connotation might be."

"Of course, I'd get on the horse. I'm not stupid. I'm just saying that I don't want to be perceived as someone who needs rescuing."

"Why? You think being in need of rescue equates to weakness? What would you call the male equivalent of a damsel in distress?"

Wisps of a cloud floated across the moon, dimming what little light we had. The accompanying breeze lifted the edges of the blanket, and I hugged it tighter around me.

"There's really not an equivalent. In traditional story constructs, the male is always the hero. Automatically. He portrays the strength, the power, the brawn. The female is often put into some dire situation, and the male swoops in and rescues her to demonstrate his masculinity."

"Hmm. Interesting." He crossed his arms over his chest. "Suddenly, I'm not sure how to feel about myself. Here I was, in dire need of rescue, and a female hero swooped in and dragged me out. I *was* feeling grateful, but now that I realize it's a negative to need rescuing and pretty much unheard of to be a dude in distress, I'm sort of conflicted about the whole thing. Perhaps she should have left me to die with my masculinity intact rather than have me wrestle with the knowledge that I needed someone's help."

Even in the darkness, I could see the teasing twinkle of mirth in his eyes and the hint of a grin playing at the corners of his mouth, but I struggled to find enjoyment in our banter when our lives were still very much in danger.

"I wasn't insinuating...I was just...you know what, never mind. It hurts my throat to talk."

"You should drink more water. You need to stay hydrated and flush the toxins from your system." He picked up a bottle from the supply stash and offered it to me.

I shook my head. "No. I'm fine. We don't have a lot, and we need to make it last."

"If you need it, drink it. Holding onto it won't help if you can't breathe or can't swallow."

"I said I'm fine. Did you find any other supplies?"

"No. You did good; you got everything worth saving." He tossed the water bottle back on the ground near the other supplies and then looked back at me. "How are you feeling? Honestly. I want the truth. Not what you feel like you should say for perception."

"I'm okay, all things considered. My lungs hurt. My throat hurts.

My head is pounding. I bet I'll be sore as hell once the adrenaline starts to wane, but for now, I'm okay."

He took a few steps away from me and looked up at the sky, dragging his hand across his face with a deep sigh. He shook his head and then kicked at the dirt, and I wondered what was weighing so heavily on him.

A sense of dread crept over me, and I asked even though I wasn't sure I wanted the answer.

"What's wrong?"

He didn't answer, and the longer he paused, the more trepidation I felt.

"What?" I pressed. "What are you thinking?"

With another sigh, he turned back to me. "We definitely veered off course for the last part of the flight, but I'm certain the pilots would have communicated our location before we went down. That'll narrow down the search area. It won't take long for them to get a team in the air to look for us. In fact, they could already be on their way now. They'll likely find the other crash site first, but the tail section couldn't have traveled too far on its own. It'll be daylight in a couple of hours, so when they come looking, it shouldn't take them long to find you."

"To find *me*? Where will you be?"

He grimaced and shifted his weight from one foot to the other. "I have to go find Kirby."

Fear, anger, and disbelief converged in my chest like three raging rivers meeting.

"What? Are you freaking kidding me? You have a head injury that knocked you unconscious for *hours*. Even now, you don't know that you might not have a brain bleed or swelling. The last thing you need to do is tromp through the dark running after some fugitive. I didn't bust my ass getting you out of that plane so you could wander off into the woods and die."

"I understand that, but I made a promise—"

"I think under the circumstances, whoever you made it to will understand. Your plane crashed, Brick. You have a head injury. No one's going to fault you for not doing your job."

"This has nothing to do with my job. This is a promise I made, and I intend to keep it." He walked toward me, closing the distance between us. "Look, I appreciate what you did. I can't thank you enough for saving my life. But that boy is going to make a huge mistake if he runs again. A mistake that will likely send him to prison for a long time, and that's if he doesn't get himself killed before they catch him."

"And what about you? What if you go and get yourself killed searching for him? How does that help him? Or anyone else, for that matter?"

"I won't. You don't need to worry about me."

"You don't know that!"

My fists were clenched so tightly that my fingernails dug into my palms. I'd never been more frightened, frustrated, and pissed off all at the same time. I wanted to punch him in the face. I wanted to shove him as hard as I could. I wanted to scream and rage and curse.

And at the same time, I wanted to cry. I wanted to throw my arms around him and plead with him not to leave me in the damned darkness all alone.

The thought of sitting there by myself with only corpses for company terrified me. And beyond the horror of being stranded in the dark with death was the reality that in the hours I sat waiting for a rescue crew to reach me, the insatiable creatures who might be watching even now from the sidelines would likely find me first.

I hated feeling vulnerable. I hated being scared. I hated that I was helpless to stop Brick from doing something so stupid. And I hated him for abandoning me, so I lashed out at him with my words.

"Fine. Go. Run after Kirby, and if you keel over in the woods with your brain pressing against your skull, you have no one to blame but yourself."

"If my brain is truly pressing against my skull, it won't matter where I am. Sitting here won't make that issue go away." His voice was so quiet and calm that it was maddening.

I'd never hit anyone in my entire life, but it took everything in me not to swing my fist at him. I even imagined what it would feel like for my knuckles to make contact with his jawbone, and though I knew it would likely hurt like hell, I reasoned that it would probably be worth the pain.

"Then go," I gritted out through clenched teeth before I lost all control and did something ridiculously stupid.

Hot tears filled my eyes and I spun away from him, not willing to let him see my vulnerability. I wanted to stalk away, but there was really no escape that wouldn't make me more miserable. I wasn't about to go back to the plane, nor did I care to take myself deeper into the woods.

"Lauryn," he said behind me, his voice soft.

My tears were coming full force now, even though I had squeezed my eyes shut against them. I wrapped my arms around my body to try to contain its trembling, but it was too late. I had reached a breaking point in my exhausted and terrified state, and I feared at any second I might explode from the inside. The last thing I wanted was a witness to my meltdown.

"Just go, dammit! Go! Get away from me!"

I felt him move closer behind me, and I stiffened, knowing that if he touched me, I would lose all control. I wasn't sure if that meant I would punch him, knee him in the nuts, or throw myself in his arms and sob, but none of those seemed like ideal scenarios.

"I mean it, Brick. Just go. Leave already."

My voice betrayed me, breaking under the strain.

"Lauryn, c'mon," he whispered, his voice soft and his breath warm on my hair. He was closer than I'd realized. "I don't want to go. I wouldn't leave if the kid wasn't in danger and if I wasn't certain that you can take care of yourself. You have more fight and determination in you than most men I've come up against. You're going to be okay."

I stepped away from him, needing to put distance between us

before my traitorous body gave into its longing and collapsed into his arms. With a last-ditch effort at composure, I turned to face him, my chin still trembling but lifted.

"I know I will be. I already told you to go. I'll be fine."

His lips pressed together in a grim line, his brows dipping low over his eyes as he drew in a deep breath. "If I'm able to find a way to get the word out, to communicate with the outside world, I'll send help as soon as I can."

I tried to memorize every feature and every detail as he stood staring at me with his head tilted slightly to one side. I studied the strong line of his jaw. The way his thick, wavy hair fell across his forehead. The crinkles at the edges of his eyes. The fullness of his bottom lip.

Underlying every other fear that held me in its grip was the realization that I would likely never see him again. It had been inevitable that at some point our time would come to an end, but I'd somehow thought that what we had experienced together had created some sort of bond. That it had tied us together in some way.

How foolish I'd been! I'd concocted this imaginary connection with a man who'd been unconscious and unaware of my feelings toward him. Now he was prepared to continue on with his life, not caring that mine had been forever changed. And if he was willing to walk away and leave me behind like this, then the attraction I'd sensed had truly been one-sided.

It hurt being wrong.

"What if you don't find him? There's nothing but woods out there and it's pitch-dark."

"True." He shoved his hands in his pockets and looked toward the trees. "But you said he was headed for a light on the other side of a canyon. I plan to try and figure out what he saw. Then, I'll just go in the same direction. Eventually, I'll catch up to him. I'm a tracker. It's what I do."

"When you find him, will you come back here?" I asked, my tone more pleading than I'd intended.

"It depends on where I find him and how long it takes. He's had a couple of hours head start, and I don't know what I'm going to encounter out there. Or how fast I'll be able to go." He reached up and touched his bandages and frowned. "I'm definitely not operating at one-hundred percent, that's for sure."

"All the more reason for you not to do this."

An uncomfortable silence stretched between us as we stood staring at each other, and when I couldn't take it any longer, I spoke to break it.

"Well, then you better get going."

He nodded once. "I think you should stay as close to the tail section as you can. It will be easier to spot you from the air in the clearing, and if any...well, if you need to hide, it would be best to be able to duck into the galley."

"Hide?" I was confused for a moment, wondering why on earth I would hide from the search crew, but then it dawned on me. "Oh, you mean if wild animals decide to attack me and tear me apart for breakfast."

"I didn't...I don't..." He grimaced and rubbed his hand across his face again. "In the rarest of chances that an animal was to get close, you make yourself as big and loud and threatening as you can be. And if that's not working, you lock yourself in that lavatory. That might give you enough of a barrier to keep you alive until help arrives."

"Right," I said, unable to believe my life had reached a point where this was a necessary topic of discussion. "You know, I've never given much thought to how I might die, but I must say that being attacked by a bear while I'm in an airplane toilet was definitely not on the list for consideration. The notion is all at once terrifying, humiliating, and laughable."

"It's not going to happen," he said, and though his voice was firm with conviction, I didn't feel reassured.

"You'll need supplies." I inclined my head toward the pile of what Kirby had left behind in an attempt to change the subject.

"I won't take much."

"Take what you need." I crossed my arms and focused on the anger, willing it to overpower the fear. "After all, I'll be rescued soon, right? You'll be the one out in the cold, wandering around chasing your tail."

I knew I was being petulant, punishing him though he'd done nothing wrong. He wasn't responsible for me or my feelings, and he owed me nothing. He'd saved my life; I'd saved his. We were square. But the anger was the only thing holding my fear at bay, and I worried that if I let go of it, I'd descend into hysteria.

EIGHT

Brick refused to take more than the bare minimum of supplies, and he wouldn't leave until we'd moved what remained along with the blanket to a spot closer to the wreckage for me. His reasoning made sense, so I did it without protest, but I did insist on moving behind the tail of the plane so I didn't have to sit and stare at the carnage up front.

"If you hear a helicopter, do whatever you can to make yourself visible," he said once we had everything settled several feet from the tail. "If it's still dark out, use your phone's flashlight to signal them. If it's daylight, wave the blanket over your head once you see them."

I nodded as I paced back and forth, swinging my arms. I couldn't stand still. With his departure imminent, my entire body buzzed with nervous energy. I'd struggled with a lifelong fear of the dark, and I was about to be stranded alone in the darkest night I'd ever encountered. I was terrified.

What if no rescue crew came? What if they didn't find me? What if I ran out of water before they did?

My mind tormented me with vivid images of my body rotting

away alone and frightened on the mountainside, and no matter how hard I tried to redirect my thoughts, it proved impossible.

That wasn't even the worst possible outcome, though. *What if I was eaten alive instead?*

I wanted to beg Brick not to go. I wanted to plead with him to stay by my side and protect me, but I hated how helpless that request made me feel, and I doubted he would stay anyway. He seemed hell-bent on completing his mission, and why would he allow a stranger he barely knew to deter him from it?

So, when the time came to say goodbye, I forced myself to put on a mask of nonchalance. I couldn't manage anything near a smile, but I didn't cry, so I considered that a win.

"Take care of yourself," Brick said, his face drawn and his mouth set in a firm frown. "Stay alert. Stay watchful. I'll send help as soon as I find a way, but I'm certain they're already aware and on it. They'll come soon. Don't worry."

"Worry? Me? No." The tears I could hold back; the sarcasm, I could not. "What do I have to worry about? I'm golden. Never better. I think as soon as the sun comes up, I'll snuggle up under the blanket and read a book on my phone. This is great, actually. I'm always wishing I had more time to read, and here I am with time on my hands and nothing else to do. Other than stay alive, of course."

"You're going to be okay," he said with quick nod. "They'll come soon. You'll go home. You'll be fine."

I wondered if his reassurance was meant for me or for him.

Did he feel any guilt at all for leaving me? Did it bother him on any level to think we may never see each other again? Or had I imagined the connection altogether?

"Goodbye, Lauryn." His grimace appeared tormented, and I got some small satisfaction from thinking that perhaps something about going bothered him after all.

"Goodbye, Brick." I held my voice steady though I felt like I was about to burst out of my skin. The terror and anxiety were so over-whelming it was all I could do not to jump up and wrap my arms around his shoulders and my legs around his waist and insist he take me with him. "You never said before—is Brick a family name? It's so unique."

The fact that I could manage mundane small talk amazed me. I suppose it served to delay his departure and offer me a distraction from the inevitable. It helped that I really was curious about the origin of his name.

If the question or its triviality in the moment surprised him, he didn't let on. "It's a nickname that kind of stuck and took on a life of its own."

"Who gave it to you?"

"Some buddies. I don't remember exactly who started it, to be honest. But they all called me that after a while."

"Why Brick?"

He paused and looked toward the sky, and I thought perhaps he wasn't going to answer, but then he chuckled.

"I don't know. I've been called that so long I haven't thought about why in a while. It probably depends on who you ask. I suppose they thought I was stubborn. Dense. Unmovable."

"Sounds like your friends weren't very fond of you. And you chose to accept this as your identity?"

He grinned and ran his hand along the back of his neck. "Why does it have to be a negative thing? They knew I was solid. That I wouldn't back down or crack under pressure. They could depend on me."

"Were you military?"

His grin faded. "Law enforcement."

"You're a cop? But I thought—"

"I was a cop. I'm not anymore."

I nodded, tucking that tidbit away in my mental file labeled *Facts about Brick.*

"So, what's your real name?"

He had been looking toward the woods, and when I asked, he looked back at me, his expression somber. "Brick."

"No, really. What was your name before that? Like, your born name."

His face clouded into a grimace. "It doesn't matter who I was before. Brick is who I am now. I gotta go. Take care of yourself, and thanks again...for everything."

Panic seized my chest. For a brief moment, I'd been so absorbed in finding out about him that I'd pushed aside the reality of his leaving. The reprieve had ended, though, and as he stepped past me to depart, I struggled once again to keep from grabbing ahold of him.

The clouds had cleared the moon, giving me enough light to see him walk across the small crash clearing and into the trees in the same direction Kirby had gone.

But as soon as he disappeared from view, it was as though the world grew infinitely darker, even though the moon still shone above me. The woods around me played a sinister symphony of sounds, and each crack, pop, and creak made me even more certain my demise was imminent.

My tormented mind even began to entertain fears of ghosts and spirits as I wondered whether those whose lives had ended might be resentful that mine had been spared. I didn't dare look toward the front of the wreckage for fear that I'd see an apparition, or even worse, an entire group of them, all seeking vengeance from me.

With my pulse racing, I closed my eyes and tried to focus on deep breathing, but that left me feeling even more vulnerable. I wanted to escape. To run. To hide. But there was no safe harbor. Certainly not the woods, which were filled with very real dangers. And the wreckage was something from a nightmare cloaked in a toxic cloud.

I looked toward the sky, praying the sun would soon rise and eliminate the darkness. The prospect of hours ahead of me waiting alone for a rescue that may or may not come suddenly seemed a fate most unbearable.

I no longer cared if I came across as weak, or helpless, or hysterical. Why had I not begged Brick to stay when I had the chance?

He hadn't been gone long. Undoubtedly, he couldn't have gotten too far. Perhaps if I yelled for him, he would hear me.

I turned back to where he'd entered the woods, stunned to see him walking toward me.

"Brick!" Rushing forward, I threw my arms around his neck, nearly knocking him to the ground with my exuberance. I didn't care if it seemed weird or inappropriate or too familiar. I clung to his solid strength; my eyes squeezed shut as my tears flowed.

"Hey, hey. It's okay. You're okay," he said, wrapping his arms around me so tightly I felt sheltered from everything around us.

"I'm sorry," I whispered against his neck. "I'm trying to be strong. To be tough. I thought I could do it. I thought I'd be fine without you here, but I'm not. I'm not! Please don't leave me here all by myself."

"I won't." His hands stroked up and down my back, soothing my sobs as I released all my pent-up emotion. "Shh. It's okay. I'm here. I'm not going anywhere. You're okay. I won't let anything happen to you."

When my hysteria was spent, I began to loosen my grip on him, but his arms remained firmly ensconced around my waist.

"Why'd you come back?" I asked, my voice thick with tears and emotion.

"I couldn't just leave you here. I'd never forgive myself if something happened to you while I was gone."

I pulled back to look up at him. "But what about Kirby? What about your promise?"

"I made a promise to you as well. I told you I'd do everything I could to make sure you get out of this okay, and this is me keeping that promise. Once I know you're safe, I'll go find Kirby."

He still hadn't released me, and it began to feel awkward to be in his embrace, so I pulled away and stepped back to straighten my skirt, suddenly feeling shy.

"Sorry," I mumbled. "I let my fears get the best of me for a minute there. I'm not a fan of the dark. Never have been."

"You don't have anything to apologize for," Brick said, his voice soft and its timbre so deep that it seemed to rumble in my very core. "Even if you were fine with the dark, these are extraordinary circumstances. I'd say you'd be hard-pressed to find anyone who wouldn't be unsettled being out here alone with things being what they are."

I stepped farther away, uncomfortable with my show of emotion and his tenderness regarding it.

"What did Kirby do, anyway?"

Brick sighed and rubbed his hand over his neck. "Kirby was in the wrong place at the wrong time with the wrong people, a recurring event in his life. That boy has always known how to find trouble. On his own, he's a good kid, but he runs with a rough crowd, and he makes bad choices."

"How long have you known each other?"

"I'd say around ten years now. He and his mother, Susan, have an apartment in the same building as mine. Susan's a good egg. Very caring lady. Hard-working single mom who's done all she can to keep a roof over Kirby's head and food in his belly, which unfortunately kept her away from home working two jobs. And he's repaid her efforts with a rap sheet two miles long. Started out with stupid stuff that kids do when they lack supervision. Graffiti. Vandalism. Destruction of property. But then he graduated into burglary, and unfortunately, doing a few stints in jail hasn't stopped him." Brick shook his head slowly with a sigh, his expression troubled. "This time, he's in way over his head. Susan contacted me three weeks ago. Said Kirby was in trouble again. They want to question him in connection with a murder."

"Murder?" My jaw dropped in shock. *The person I'd been casually interacting with had murdered someone?*

"Kirby didn't kill anyone," Brick said, waving his hand in dismissal. "The boy doesn't have it in him. He was running with some folks who decided to rob a house. The homeowner returned unexpectedly and interrupted the burglary. Kirby says he tussled with the guy while trying to get out, but he swears the man was still alive when he left. He must have been shot once Kirby was gone."

"So, then why do the cops think Kirby did it?"

"Because his dumb ass turned up at a pawn shop with jewelry that had been taken from the house. With nothing else to go on, he became their prime suspect. Rather than meeting with the cops and telling them what he knew, Kirby ran. As far as Susan knows, they aren't aware he's out of state yet. And if I can't get him back before they find out, he's going to make a bad situation a whole lot worse."

"But Kirby was there. Kirby was part of the reason someone is dead." I was still shocked that I'd been in the company of someone so closely involved in careless murder. He'd invited me to come along into the woods with him. *What if I had gone?*

"Yes, he was." Brick nodded. "I'm sure he didn't know someone was going to die, but when you ride with that kind of crew, you have to know it's a possibility. And just by having the stolen goods in his possession, he's violating probation. He's going back to jail no matter what, but if he's telling the truth, and I believe he is, then he shouldn't do time for a murder he didn't commit. And he shouldn't suffer the consequences alone when he didn't act alone."

"I'm surprised his mom asked you to bring him home, knowing that it means he'll go back to jail."

"Susan is heartbroken, for sure, and like any mother, she doesn't want to see her son locked up. But the cops aren't the only ones looking for him. You can bet his so-called friends don't want him talking and telling what he knows. I need to get him back and in protective custody before someone else finds him."

"But you had him. You found him. Why didn't you just turn him over to the cops then?"

Brick swore, twisting his lips as he let out a sharp exhale. "Because I promised Susan I'd give her a chance to talk to him before he turns himself in. She's always watched out for me. For my place. I got in a spot of trouble one night a few years ago, and she nursed me back to health, no questions asked. I told her then I owed her for one of my lives, and now, she's cashing in on the debt. I had to pull in more favors and strings than you can imagine to take a wanted murder suspect on a commercial flight in handcuffs without a badge. There's no way I'm gonna just let him disappear after all that. I owe too many people at this point. It's personal on several levels."

I took a deep breath and considered the weight he was carrying and the ramifications of my actions. Without having a clue what it meant, I had watched Kirby walk away—not that I would have been able to stop him—but now, because of me, Brick felt unable to pursue him.

It seemed an odd twist of fate that Kirby would survive a plane crash just to go to jail, but it sounded like he deserved to pay the price for his actions. And if his testimony could ensure the ones responsible for an innocent man's murder also paid, then that was all the more reason he needed to be brought back.

A battle ensued inside my head as I weighed what felt right against what felt safe. I bit down hard on my lip, trying to hold back the words I knew I was about to speak.

"Let's go find him."

NINE

Brick's head jerked up and his eyes widened in surprise. "What?"

"You can't just let him get away. He needs to suffer the consequences of his actions, and he needs to bring the others to justice. The longer you wait to go after him, the more of a head start he gets. Let's go find him."

"You can't seriously be suggesting that we go together."

"Why not? I can't stay here any longer, Brick. I'm about to lose my mind, I swear. I want to get away from all this death. If we can find that house Kirby saw, I can call my parents and let them know we're okay."

"Lauryn, the chances of there being any phone service in this remote—"

"But he said there were lights. That means there's electricity. That means warmth!"

"Not necessarily. This far out? Those outside lights are probably run by a solar panel. It's likely nothing more than a hunting cabin."

"I don't care. If it's got a roof and walls, it would be better than being out here in the woods hoping we don't become bear breakfast.

And even if it's a hunting cabin, it has to have some kind of road leading to it. If we can follow the road once it's daylight, we could find other people."

"That's a whole lot of *ifs* in one sentence. Look, let's just do what we can to be comfortable here. It's best for us to remain with the fuselage. That's the easiest, quickest way to be found."

"Yeah, well, we're already not at the main crash site, so it's going to be harder for them to find us anyway. I say we take our chances on making it to a phone before they make it to us."

"You have no idea what may lie between us and that cabin. You're not dressed for hiking." He nodded toward my shoes. "Especially not in those heels."

Sticking my foot out, I turned my ankle left and right with my cute leather sandals on display. "I'm accustomed to walking in heels. I wear heels every day."

"I'd wager you don't wear them in the woods where there are tree roots, gopher holes, and God only knows what other hazards."

My resolve wavered, but I refused to let him see my doubt. "It'll be fine. I can keep up, I swear."

"I'm not concerned about you keeping up. I'm worried you're gonna twist your ankle or fall and break your leg."

"Well, I'm not concerned about either of those things," I lied. "I'm ready. Let's do this."

"What if we have to cross a creek?"

I shivered at the thought of being in frigid water, but my mind was made up. "I'm telling you, I can't sit here any longer. I need to be on the move. I need to feel like I'm heading toward a solution rather than sitting here hoping someone else is headed toward me. Let's try it. I promise you won't hear a single complaint out of me."

His expression said he doubted that was true, and to be honest, I doubted it myself, but I was tired of feeling antsy and trapped and helpless. Moving towards a goal, towards a target, would give me something to focus on.

"This is not going to be easy," he said, his frown clouding his entire face. "It's still dark out for a couple more hours, and it'll be hard to see where we're walking. Plus, the trail isn't the only thing we have to worry about. We might encounter those bears you keep talking about. Coyotes. Bobcats."

"My dad always told me they're more scared of us than we are of them, and the key to getting them to leave you alone is to make yourself as threatening as possible. Well, the two of us together make for formidable prey, don't you think?"

He took a few steps away from me and put his hands on his hips as he stared into the woods. I knew he wanted to go. He was likely itching to get on Kirby's trail and recapture him. He'd been torn between two promises when he returned to stay by my side, and this plan allowed him to fulfill both.

"It'll be daylight soon," I said, hoping to nudge him. "You won't be able to see the lights to guide us then. We should go now."

Looking over his shoulder at me, he frowned and then turned back to the woods. "I try to never do anything I think I might regret, and I don't see any way I won't regret this."

"More than you'd regret letting Kirby get away?" I nudged harder.

"Stay here." He wandered a little farther into the woods and returned with two large sticks, handing one to me. "Is that too heavy? Can you swing it?"

I took a couple of practice swings, widening my stance to counterbalance the weight of it. "Yeah. I think so."

"Okay. Let's hope you don't need to."

He grabbed the supplies he'd gathered before and added them to what remained, placing it all in the center of the blanket. Then he tied the ends together around the stick I'd held earlier, creating a bindle he could sling over his shoulder.

"You sure about this?" he asked once he was done. "We can stay here. I don't want you to feel like you have to go."

"No. I want to."

"If you change your mind, if you want to turn back—"

"I won't." I shook my head and then stared at him with a lifted chin. "When I make up my mind to reach a goal, I don't quit."

His eyes met mine and held them for a moment, and that now familiar jolt danced across my skin. I wished I hadn't been so near hysterical when I'd been in his arms earlier. I'd been too distracted to get the full effect of what it was like to be held by him, and I wondered if I'd ever get the chance again.

"All right. Let's go. I swear I must have lost my damn mind when I got hit in the head," he muttered as he moved past me toward the point where Kirby had gone.

I followed along behind him, happy at first to feel as though I'd won a battle, but as we began our trek into the darkness, fear and trepidation gripped me once more.

I'd always hated the dark and not knowing what I couldn't see. The concept of what might be there that I was unaware of. When my cousins had all insisted on playing hide-and-seek outside in our youth, I'd always opted to hide near the house or one of the barns, closer to the lights. Growing up, Dani and Piper had both teased me about being scared of the dark, and they'd been relentless in their efforts to hide behind things to jump out and scare me.

But the fears I'd had then had been trivial compared to now. Back then, I was surrounded by those I loved and in a relatively safe environment. Now, the mountain forest was filled with unknown dangers, and it was darker than anywhere I'd ever been. It wasn't just difficult to see. It was impossible.

And yet, Brick forged ahead, seemingly unfazed by his surroundings and steady in his path as though he were following some invisible trail. Occasionally, he would click on the tiny light on his keychain and survey the area with it, but then he'd turn it off and trudge on.

"Be careful with your footing," he said. "These leaves have rotted beneath the snow when it melted, so they're slick, and there are roots sticking out everywhere."

"Got it. I'm basically just trying to step wherever you step, since I can't really see the ground anyway."

I'd noticed that it was slippery in spots, and I'd stumbled over a root a couple of times already, but I hadn't mentioned it because I didn't want him to change his mind about our trek.

"You all right?" he asked once we'd journeyed a bit farther.

"Yeah. You? We can stop and rest whenever you need to, you know? You don't want to overdo it with a head injury. How are you feeling?"

"I'm okay," he answered as he moved a branch aside for me to pass. "I have a headache, of course, which is to be expected. I'm a little dizzy and a little nauseous, but that could easily be due to lack of sustenance as much as the injury."

"You never did eat anything, did you? You want some cookies? Pretzels?"

"Not yet. Those are both snacks provided with the intention of encouraging you to purchase beverages, so until my stomach protests to the point that I can't keep going, I don't want to eat something that's just going to make me thirstier."

Talking made the dark more bearable, so I asked a question to keep the conversation going.

"You said you were in law enforcement before, but now you're a ...what did you call it...fugitive—"

"Fugitive recovery agent."

"Right. Is that the same thing as a bounty hunter?"

"Pretty much."

"So, how'd you go from being a cop to being a bounty hunter?"

"It's a long story."

"Well, what do you know? I happen to have some time on my hands. I'm all ears."

He shot me a glance and paused before continuing. "Let's just say that my objective is to bring the bad guys to justice. Sometimes, following the rules of law conflicts with that objective, so I've been known to bend the rules."

"What does that mean? You broke the law? What did you do?"

"I wasn't willing to let guilty people walk away. I worked a case where I knew a suspect was guilty. He'd assaulted a girl, and he was going to get away with it. He admitted it to me and my partner, but it was inadmissible in court. So, I ensured there was enough evidence to make sure the case stuck."

"You fabricated evidence?"

"No. The evidence was already there. We just didn't have the proper search warrant to find it. So, I moved it to a more convenient place."

"And you got caught?"

"No. Well, yes. My chief knew what I'd done, and why I'd done it. He didn't disagree with the outcome, but he couldn't support my methods. We decided it would be mutually agreeable for me to leave the department. I have no regrets. It was worth my badge to see that asshole in prison."

"Don't bounty hunters have to follow the law?"

"Sure. But it's easier to bend the rules when there are less people watching."

"So, what made you wanna chase bad guys for a living?"

"You ask a lot of questions."

I chuckled. "That's what my mom always says. She calls me and my brother chatterboxes. When we were younger, she'd tell us to go to our rooms and stay until she told us to come out just so she could get some peace and quiet."

"You just have the one brother then? Or do you have other siblings who were much quieter and couldn't get a word in?"

Thoughts of my family brought back the horror of our situation, and I wondered if they thought I was dead. I knew my mother would never give up on finding me until she'd seen my body for herself. But if search crews found the ashes Kirby had described, they'd assume I was among the dead. After all, my assigned seat was in that section of the plane that Kirby said had been completely destroyed.

Guilt for their unnecessary suffering fell over me like a dark cloud, and a huge lump formed in my throat.

What on earth was I doing hiking through the darkness with a rogue bounty hunter chasing what may be a dangerous criminal? Why wasn't I trying to find the main crash site so I would be able to signal a search crew and let them know I was alive?

"Hey," Brick said. He had stopped and turned to face me, and I nearly bumped into him. "You okay?"

"Yeah," I said, shaking my head to dispel the unwanted images of my devastated loved ones. "Just thinking of my family."

He lifted his hand as though he were going to caress my cheek, but then he hesitated and let it fall. "You're going to see them soon. We'll let them know you're okay as soon as we can."

"What if the search crew comes while we're gone? What if they see what's left of the plane and tell my family I didn't survive before we get in touch with them? I can't imagine what my parents must be going through. My grandparents. My brother. My cousins. I want them to know I'm okay. I don't want them to think I'm...that I..."

My eyes filled with tears again, and this time, Brick didn't hesitate as he wrapped his arms around me and pulled me to his chest.

"We can turn back," he said, his voice rumbling in his chest as I laid my ear against it. "Or we can try and find the other crash site if that's what you want to do."

I considered his offer and was tempted to agree that it would be the right choice. But there was no way of knowing how long it would take the search team to come, and the entire time we were waiting, Kirby could be getting farther away.

"No," I shook my head, squaring my shoulders as I pulled away from his embrace. "Let's find Kirby and a way to call my parents."

We'd only walked a little farther when we came to the edge of a wide valley. On the other side, almost directly across from us, two amber lights twinkled in the trees, sparking a tiny sprig of hope in my chest.

"There! There are the lights Kirby saw," I said, pointing. "That's got to be a house, right? There's no other reason there would be random lights out here."

"It does appear to be manmade."

I glared at him for his lack of enthusiasm. "Well, yeah. I didn't think fairies built it. If they have lights, they probably have electricity, right? How long will it take us to reach it?"

Rubbing his hand across the stubble on his chin, he let out a low whistle. "The valley's not deep, but it's wide. Hard to say." He looked down at my shoes and grimaced. "Several hours at least. Maybe even a day."

"No! Seriously? We can do it quicker than that. Come on! Where's your optimism?"

"I've always been more of a realist than an optimist."

Frowning, I crossed my arms over my chest. "How can you say that? Weren't you the one on the plane telling me we were going to be fine? You were confident we'd survive. If I remember correctly, you said, '*I've got more lives than an alley cat.*' If that's not optimism, I don't know what is!"

"I didn't say that because I'm an optimist, Lauryn. I said that because I'm cursed. I survive things no one should."

"How can you say that's a curse? Would you rather be dead?"

He had already turned away from me and moved toward the drop-off in front of us, surveying the ground. "Sometimes, yes. I would. There's no safe place for us to head down here. It's too steep. You're going to break your neck in those damned heels."

I had opened my mouth to question why on earth he'd say he'd rather be dead, and then he made the comment about my heels, and I reformulated my response to fit that. But before I said anything, I joined him at the edge of the drop-off and looked down. I closed my mouth, gulping at the rugged terrain below us. I don't know that I could have navigated it in hiking boots, much less a flimsy pair of leather, heeled sandals.

"Okay, that's intense," I said. "There has to be an easier way down, right?"

"Not necessarily." He continued to move along the edge of the valley. "It's not like this is a park with marked trails. We're talking wilderness here."

"So, what do we do?"

Brick chewed on his lip as he stood with his hands on his hips, the valley sweeping behind him as the moon peeked through the clouds. He looked like a rugged model for some hipster clothing company or an upscale cologne ad, and an insane part of me wished I could just walk up to him, wrap my arms around his neck, and press my lips to his, distracting us both from the absurdity of our situation.

"We turn back," he said, releasing a huge sigh.

TEN

"No. Not yet. We can't just give up at the first sign of a difficult path. Let's walk a little farther and see if there's a way down."

"Lauryn—"

"We have to at least try, Brick. What if we turn back now and there's the perfect opportunity just up ahead? I mean, Kirby had to go down somewhere, right? And there's no sign of anyone going through here. So maybe he found a better way, and we could too."

"It's not safe."

"Nothing that has happened to me so far tonight has been safe! I need to keep moving. I need to feel like we're actively progressing toward home. Otherwise, my mind will meander down all the rabbit holes, and I'm going to fall apart." I stepped closer to him, my voice starting to break with the intensity of my plea. "Please, Brick. Let's go a little farther. If we haven't found a way, in say...a half hour, then we can talk about turning back."

He stared down at me for a moment and then swore. "I get the feeling I'm not the only one who's as stubborn to talk to as a brick wall."

"My grandma always said I was as stubborn as a mule. I prefer to think of myself as tenacious and determined. I don't give up easily."

"I've noticed," he said, turning to continue alongside the valley.

I smiled, knowing I'd won the battle. For now. Feeling confident, I tackled another battle issue in hopes of winning again.

"Why won't you tell me your real name?"

"I did tell you...it's Brick."

"Is that your legal name? Like, if I asked to see your driver's license, would it say *Brick*?"

"You're not going to let this go, are you?"

He didn't seem defensive or perturbed, so I pushed the issue, my curiosity piqued even more by his efforts to dodge the question.

"It must be awful if you won't tell me. What if I guess? Will you tell me if I guess?"

"No."

"Percival...Poindexter...Bartholomew...Claxton."

He looked over his shoulder at me with his forehead scrunched. "Where the hell are you coming up with these names? You know people with names like that?"

"Can't you just tell me? I won't tell anyone, I swear. And it's not like we know any of the same people anyway. Who am I gonna tell that would matter?"

"Lauryn, my name is Brick. Plain and simple."

"No, it's not. You already said it's a nickname. Are you worried I'll laugh? I promise I won't. Is it Clancy? Ralph? Theodore?"

"Hey—I had an uncle named Theodore. It's a solid name."

"Is that it? Is it Theodore? Were you named after your uncle?"

"No. Look," he said, turning to face me as he stopped walking. "My name's Brick. End of story. Let's talk about something else."

"Okay, fine." I held up my hands in surrender and he began to walk again. "Sheesh. What do you want to talk about?"

"You're the one who wants to talk. Tell me something about your life."

"My life's boring. There's nothing to tell."

"Somehow I doubt that. Where were you flying to?"

"Home." I frowned at the thought of not making it there. "I was coming home from a book convention."

He turned, one eyebrow raised. "You're an author?"

"No, a reader. I went to meet authors, buy books, and hang out in person with reader friends I usually only get to see online."

"And how was that?"

"It was awesome. I got to have lunch with one of my favorite authors. I had custard for the first time with a reader group who call themselves the RCC, and I shared a room with some friends from the Literary Poptarts, a chat group I'm in. And of course, I came home with way too many—"

I stopped short as I considered the fate of my luggage and its contents. "Oh no!"

"What's wrong?" Brick whirled to face me, his eyes searching for the source of my dismay.

"All my books! The books I bought at the event and had signed by the authors! Some were for my personal shelves, but some were for the library where I work. And now, they're gone. I mean, obviously, in the grand scheme of things, what with people dying and all, it's not that big of a deal, but—"

His eyelids drooped, and then he swayed before stumbling to one side. He grabbed hold of a tree and braced his shoulder against it as I screamed his name and rushed to help hold him upright.

"Are you okay? Brick! Are you okay?"

His eyes were closed, and he released a long, slow breath before responding.

"Sorry," he mumbled. "Got dizzy. I'll be fine in a sec."

"You need to sit down. You have to take it easy, remember? Oh, God, I wish I could call my mother and ask her what to do. You definitely have a concussion. I'm certain of it. But I don't know how to tell if it's getting worse or something. Other than vomiting, I don't know what to look for, and I have no clue what to do for it."

"And your mother would?"

The weakness in his voice alarmed me.

"Yeah, she would. My mom's a nurse. She'd know exactly what to do. She'd be able to help you. I'm gonna try again to see if I can find a signal."

I pulled my phone from my purse and powered it on, desperately hoping that we'd gotten closer to a cell tower somehow.

"That's a nice picture of you," Brick said when my screensaver photo popped up.

I rubbed my thumb across the smiling faces as my heart clenched with longing. "Thanks. Those are my cousins, Dani and Piper. My best friends for *literally* my entire life. My family called us the Three Musketeers when we were younger."

"You have a close family, huh?"

"Yeah. Really close." I frowned as the words *No Service* appeared at the top of the screen. "Argh. Still nothing."

Holding the phone above my head as I stared at it, I moved toward the open valley in hopes it would improve my chances of finding a tower.

"Watch where you're walking," Brick cautioned, his voice a little stronger than it had been before. "Don't get too close to the edge."

"I'm watching, I'm watching." I looked down at the ground as I replied, backing up when I realized I was a little closer to the drop-off than I had thought. "Would they be able to pick up a signal from my phone if my phone can't find a signal? What I mean is, if it's turned on, will someone be able to find a ping or whatever they call it even if I'm showing no signal? Will they be able to track us?"

"If a tower is able to pick up your phone's signal, yes. You should try sending a text. A text might go through even when a call can't."

"But if the phone says *No Service*—"

I had turned back toward Brick as I spoke, and I froze as I stared into the eyes of the large coyote standing no more than twenty feet behind him.

The blood seemed to drain from my head, and I couldn't think. I couldn't even form words to warn Brick, but the tension rolling off me must have been palpable, because he began to turn slowly in the direction of my gaze.

The coyote broke eye contact with me to watch Brick, and my fear of the animal was outweighed by my fear of what he might do to Brick as he sat vulnerable and weakened underneath the tree.

Having grown up in rural Florida, I'd always been taught that the best defense against a lone coyote was to go on the offense. I drew myself up as tall as I could manage and began to wave my arms and shout. I stalked forward past Brick, scooping up the stick I'd dropped when I'd knelt by his side earlier.

Swinging the stick back and forth like a bat, I roared like a mad woman as the coyote spread his front legs wide and dipped his head. He looked left and right as though he were weighing his options and how big of a threat I might be. He must have determined I was either dangerous or crazy—maybe both—because he turned and ran, and within seconds, the darkness of the woods had swallowed him up and he was no longer visible.

My entire body trembled with adrenaline as I turned and looked at Brick, who stood behind me with one hand on the tree for support and the other hand brandishing his own stick.

"He's gone," I said, my voice breathless with fear and excitement and raspy from the coughing I'd done once I finished screaming.

"I see that." Cocking his head to the side, Brick grinned. "I think I'm going to call you a warrior instead of a damsel."

"I'm good with that." I returned his smile, adding a little sass of pride to my step as I walked back toward him. "You okay? Feeling any better?"

"Yeah," he said, but neither his face nor his voice matched his answer. "I'll be fine. I think I'm gonna have a pack of those pretzels and see if that might settle my stomach a bit. You want some?"

"Don't you think we should keep moving? You know, in case that coyote goes and finds a group of friends and brings them back to settle the score?"

Just the thought of a pack of predators watching us from the woods sent a shiver up my spine, and my skin prickled all over with heightened awareness.

Brick followed my gaze toward the woods as he knelt and untied the bindle. "I don't think he wants to tangle with you again. He won't be back any time soon. Pretzels or cookies?"

He held up a packet of each.

"Cookies," I said, and he opened the bag and handed it to me.

We munched in silence for a moment, each of us lost in our own thoughts, but then the dryness of the cookies on my irritated throat triggered another coughing spell.

"That cough seems to be getting worse," Brick said, his brow crinkled with concern. "You feeling okay?"

I nodded as I tried unsuccessfully to suppress the urge. I'd been coughing somewhat frequently the entire time we'd been walking, and I feared he was right in thinking it was getting worse instead of better. My ribs hurt from the force and the repetition, and my throat, which had been raw since the initial smoke exposure after the crash, stayed irritated without enough time between spells to rest and recuperate. My voice was growing hoarser from it all.

To make matters worse, the temperature seemed to be dropping around us, and I hugged my arms around me, rubbing my hands up and down them as I stamped my feet to generate warmth.

"You're cold," Brick said, stating the obvious.

"It's all right. No colder than I've been all night," I lied, forcing a smile.

"If I had a coat to offer you, I would." Brick frowned as he looked down at his clothing. "Do you want my shirt?"

I shook my head, rolling my eyes at the ridiculous notion of his offer. "No! Of course not! How would it make sense for me to take your shirt and leave you walking around freezing?"

"You know, you should always travel with a jacket. And shoes that would be easy to walk in for a great distance or run in if you had to."

"You sound like my dad."

"He must be a smart man." Brick grinned.

"He is. And just so you know, I had a jacket with me, but it was in my carry-on bag. And I think I've walked pretty well in these shoes so far."

A breeze swept through the trees, and I shivered again as it brushed across my bare legs.

"C'mere," Brick said, extending his arms and motioning me forward with his hands. "I may not have an extra layer of clothes to offer you, but I can at least hold you and share my own warmth."

"That's okay," I said, shaking my head as I released my hands from my arms and tried to look less cold. "I'll be fine once we get moving again."

He dropped his arms, and I tried not to regret turning down his offer. As much as I would have enjoyed the warmth, I was certain that being in his arms again—and being awake for it this time—would only make it harder to deny the intense attraction I felt for him. It was going to be tough enough to say goodbye once we were rescued. No reason to make it more torturous for myself.

"Correct me if I'm wrong," he said, his eyes narrowing as he grinned, "but I woke to find you beneath a blanket with me. I'm assuming you did that to combine our body heat and warm us both?"

My face flushed hot with the memory of waking in his embrace, and a different kind of shiver raced across my skin, igniting a warm ember in my core. "Yeah, but that was different. You were unconscious, and you'd lost a lot of blood. That was for survival."

"True," he said, and I wondered if I was imagining that he looked disappointed by my refusal. "But these are still extraordinary circumstances, so I think we could classify close contact as a necessity for survival. Oh, and I don't think I ever did say sorry for the rather, um, amorous way I woke up. I'm more awake and aware of what's going on this time. I promise not to take any liberties if you'll let me hold you."

I bit down on my lip, struggling to maintain my resolve. The cold had seeped into my skin and felt bone-deep, and I wanted nothing more than to crush myself against his chest and have his arms envelop me in his warmth.

Could I trust myself not to have some kind of crazy emotions attached to the act? Could I just allow it to be survival and nothing more?

Did it even matter? Wouldn't it be worth it just to be held by him for any reason for any amount of time?

When we'd gone our separate ways and our lives were back to mundane routines, at least I'd have a few moments of bliss to remember in the midst of this horrific nightmare.

Releasing my lip, I sighed with a shrug. "I guess we could hold each other. I mean, for warmth. For survival. Of course."

"Right. Warmth. Survival. Nothing else."

ELEVEN

He held out his arms, and I stepped into them, holding my breath as they tightened around me and he pulled me in close.

It was even more heavenly than I remembered.

When Brick had held me earlier, I'd been frantic with worry about my family, and my emotions had leaned toward fear and overwhelming uncertainty. This time, I wasn't so distraught, which made it impossible not to be aware of how perfect he felt. How solid. How incredibly masculine.

At first, I just nestled against him with my elbows bent and my arms tucked between our chests, content to bask in the heat coming from him.

But as I relaxed into enjoying and appreciating how wonderful it was to be held by him, I sank deeper into his embrace, winding my arms around his waist and tucking my head beneath his chin. He adjusted his stance to pull me even closer, leaving no space at all between us.

I swear I could have stood there for eons. It no longer mattered that we were stranded on the side of a mountain. I didn't feel the cold or fear the darkness. It was as though the world fell away and nothing else existed beyond the two of us and the present moment.

"Better?" he asked after a while, his voice a deep rumble in his chest that vibrated against my cheek.

"Yeah," I said, leaning back to look up at him. "Thank you."

When our eyes met, the jolt hit me again, even more intense than before. His arms tightened around me, and I was certain this time that he must feel it too. *How could he not?* My skin seemed to burn everywhere my body made contact with his. Surely, a heat like that couldn't be generated all by myself.

Was this normal? Did other people feel this insane connection with one another?

I'd always brushed off the idea of instant attraction as fiction fodder in the novels I read, but this was undeniably real and like nothing I'd ever experienced before.

His gaze fell to my lips, and I held my breath in hopes he would kiss me.

It played out so vividly in my mental image reel that my lips tingled from the phantom pressure, and I sank my teeth into the fleshiest part of my bottom lip to ground myself in reality.

He lifted his eyes to mine, and I shuddered at the intensity of the desire evident there. His embrace tightened even further, and then he began to stroke one hand up and down my back, driving me insane with yearning.

"Still cold?" he asked, his voice husky.

"Not even a little bit." *Good God, man. Would you just kiss me already?*

As though he'd heard my silent demand and decided to grant my request, he bent his head and reached to cup my face in his hand. He brushed his thumb across my skin in the gentlest of caresses, and I shuddered again, grateful he was holding me as my knees went weak.

So slowly that I thought I might self-combust with anticipation, he pressed his lips to mine. Something deep in my core contracted, and this time the jolt hit much lower in my body, sending pleasurable sensations to all the right places.

He didn't move the kiss along any further, his mouth seeming shy against mine. By contrast, I was frantic with yearning, and I lifted myself onto my toes and pressed my body even closer to his, smoothing my hands across taut washboard abs and up over pecs so firm and rounded they strained against the material of his slim-fitting shirt. I brushed my tongue across his bottom lip, seeking entry, and he opened his mouth to me and then began to roll his tongue against mine.

But before the kiss deepened any farther, he went back to the close-mouthed peck on the lips where he'd began.

"Lauryn," he whispered, pulling back just far enough that we could look into each other's eyes. "I—"

He hesitated, his arms like a vice around me as we stood there staring at each other. He opened his mouth as if to say more, but then he closed it, and I needed to tell him that I understood. That the words weren't even necessary.

Moving my hands to cup his face, I smiled up at him. "I know. I feel the same way."

His eyes clouded and his brows scrunched together as he frowned. He released me so abruptly that I nearly fell forward without his weight to support me, and when he turned away, his back seemed like a solid and impenetrable wall.

The sting of rejection was colder than the air that swirled around me with his absence.

"Okay," I said, closing my arms over my chest in a belated effort to protect my heart. "Obviously, I misread that situation."

With an almost inaudible curse, he stepped farther away and then turned back to face me, his hands on his hips. "Lauryn, I'm sorry. I never should have allowed that to happen. I can't. It's just that I..."

A realization dawned, and though my pride still stung, my disappointment was tempered with understanding.

"Ah, you have a girlfriend. It's okay. I respect that. Huge respect for that, in fact. Don't worry. You have nothing to feel guilty for. It's the situation, really. That whole surviving together, being alone on the mountain in the dark. You said before, these are extenuating circumstances, right? You haven't betrayed her. Not really."

"Lauryn, there's no one else. I just can't—"

"Don't." I held up a hand to stop him from driving the dagger any deeper. His rejection was easier to swallow when I thought he'd turned away due to honor and a sense of loyalty steeped in love. I didn't want to know that he just wasn't that into me. Especially since we were still in a life and death situation, and I was literally the only option around. *Talk about insulting!*

"But I—"

"Please, Brick. It's okay. We both got caught up in the stress of the moment. Please don't give me the *'it's not you, it's me'* speech. All right? Can we skip that and just jump straight to pretending nothing ever happened?"

Rubbing his hand across the back of his neck, he swore again. "It's really not you."

"Right. I know. I get it. There's no need to discuss it further. We need to get moving anyway. Which way do we go?"

"Lauryn, you have to understand. I don't do...*this*." He pointed back and forth between us as I tried to swallow the huge lump of wounded pride lodged firmly in my tender throat. "My life...the life I've chosen..."

"Look, I get it, okay? Kirby already told me you're a loner, so you don't need to explain. Not that you owed me any explanation, because you don't. Obviously. It was a kiss between two traumatized people seeking warmth and solace in the midst of a horrific night. Nothing more. In fact, I'm fine with pretending it never happened. End of story."

"*Kirby?* What did Kirby say? When? And how in the hell did this topic come up?"

I'd said too much. To tell Brick what transpired in the conversation with Kirby, I'd have to reveal that Kirby thought we had feelings for each other. I wasn't sure I could convincingly play it off as nonsense with my heart still on my sleeve the way it was, and my bruised ego definitely wasn't up for Brick confirming that Kirby was wrong about us.

"Does it really matter? What's important right now is getting rescued. Without knowing how bad your head injury is, I don't think we should stray too far from the wreckage. I know you feel like you have to find Kirby but—"

Brick lifted his hand and gestured for me to be quiet as he stared beyond me, his entire body suddenly tense as if on high alert.

I froze, but then, terrified that something sinister was approaching behind me, I whirled with my fists clenched, wishing I still had my stick as I searched the woods for whatever new threat Brick had detected.

"What?" I asked when I saw nothing.

"Shh. Listen."

A faint whirring sound drifted across the breeze from the distance, so far away that at first it didn't register what I was hearing. But then as it got closer, the sound grew more distinctive, and I turned back to Brick in excitement.

"You hear that, right? You hear it!" I jumped up and down like a little kid on Christmas morning. "They're coming! That's a helicopter. They're looking for us!"

"It's definitely a helicopter. Whether or not they're looking for us remains to be seen, but we need to make sure they find us either way."

"They won't be able to see us under these trees. Do we have time to make it back to the tail section before they reach us?"

His jaw was tight, his mouth a grim line as he considered our options. "How much battery does your phone have left?"

I pulled it from my bag. "Thirty percent. Why? What are you going to do?"

"Use the flashlight to signal them."

"Will they be able to see that?"

"If we wait until they get close enough."

We moved to the edge of the drop-off, both of us searching for the night sky.

"I see them!" I pointed toward the distant specks of red. "There! See the lights?"

I exhaled with a giggle, giddy with relief and excitement. Maybe they had paramedics on board. Maybe they'd be able to help Brick, and if not, then perhaps they'd be able to take him to a hospital. And they were sure to have a way to communicate, so they could call my family.

The chopper was still too far away for me to be able to make out anything other than tiny lights, but knowing they were there, that they were on their way, was enough.

My relief was short-lived as the lights veered to the right.

"What are they doing? Where are they going?"

"They're circling," Brick said. "They might be looking for sign of the crash based on the last coordinates they had."

I turned back to him. "Do you think the main crash is in that direction? Would it be that far away from us?"

He leaned his shoulder against a tree and closed his eyes. Instinct made me move toward him, but he shook his head.

"I'm okay," he said, waving me back. "Keep your eye on the sky."

My capacity to worry was pulled in two different directions, but I knew the helicopter had to be my top priority. Turning away from Brick, I watched them make another circle, even wider than the first. Then they began to move back in the direction from which they came.

"No, no, no," I cried. "Come this way!"

Frantic for them to see me, I grabbed the phone from Brick and began to run along the valley's edge holding it up with the flashlight turned on, though I knew it would be impossible for them to see from such a distance, especially with them going the opposite direction.

"Lauryn, be careful!" Brick cautioned. "They'll come back. They'll find us. Just stay put and wait for them to get closer."

I didn't listen. I couldn't bear the thought of them leaving without us. I didn't want them to see ashes scattered across the ground and cause my parents even more unnecessary grief. I had to find a way to signal them.

Ignoring Brick's pleas and the sound of his footsteps behind me, I continued moving toward the lights, grabbing onto trees for balance as I ran and using the flashlight to illuminate the ground ahead of me.

"Lauryn, stop!" Brick yelled behind me. "They won't be able to see you from this far. You're going to break your neck running in those heels!"

He was no longer coming behind me, and I glanced back to see him doubled over, holding onto a tree. Once again, I felt torn, but just up ahead was a break in the trees where it appeared the bluff fell away.

"There's a clearing," I said, my lungs burning with the sudden exertion. "I think I can signal them."

My throat spasmed with a cough, and yet I kept running. It worsened, but I was so close to the clearing that I refused to stop. My side clenched with a stitch so strong it would have taken my breath away if I hadn't already been struggling to breathe.

I stumbled, and my toe caught on a root, pitching my weight forward. With my arms flailing, I tried to recover, but when I put my other foot down, the sole of my sandal slid on the rotted leaves. My ankle gave way, and I went down hard.

Unfortunately, my body's forward momentum combined with the slight downhill slope toward the bluff caused me to roll end over end. Sticks and roots battered me mercilessly as I tumbled, and then, the ground disappeared as I went over the edge.

TWELVE

The world was a slow-motion blur as I plummeted. I screamed, but my lungs and throat had nothing left to give and only a hoarse squawking sound came out.

A narrow ledge roughly twelve feet down broke my fall, the impact knocking every last bit of oxygen from me. Overwhelmed with shock and terror, I gasped for air, but no air came.

"Lauryn," Brick yelled above me. "Lauryn!"

I couldn't breathe, much less respond.

"Oh, God, Lauryn, are you all right? Please say something. Are you all right? Lauryn!"

The unperturbed calm I'd come to expect from him was gone, replaced by a distraught panic.

I lifted my left hand and attempted to wave it, hoping he'd be able to see it and know I was alive.

"I'm going to figure out a way to get to you," he said. "Just stay put. Don't move, okay?"

I gave him a thumbs up and tried to focus on breathing slowly and deeply. I'd been pitched from a horse and gotten the wind knocked out of me enough times to know that I needed to force my diaphragm to relax and do its job to push air out and in.

My right arm was killing me, but I couldn't tell if it was broken or just protesting the fact that I'd landed on it and it was now pinned beneath me with the weight of my body compressing it against the rock.

I'd landed on my side with my face toward the mountain, and without knowing how wide the ledge was, I didn't dare roll onto my back to release my arm. The last thing I wanted was to send myself hurtling toward the ground again.

I lifted my head to survey the situation, but when I turned it to look behind me, I immediately wished I hadn't.

The ledge was barely wide enough to hold me, and one wrong move would send me plummeting again. My heart began to pound so wildly I feared it would catapult out of my chest. I'd never been scared of heights, but I'd also never been stranded on a narrow strip of rock with the ground so far beneath me that I couldn't make it out in the dark.

"Are you injured?" Brick asked.

I hurt all over, but other than my right arm, the pain seemed manageable. I felt certain it was more bruises and cuts than anything life-threatening, but I did an inventory just in case I'd done serious damage.

Warily, I wiggled my left foot and then my right, wincing at the stabbing sensation the movement caused in my right ankle. Fearing it was broken, I bit down on my lip and tried moving my toes, and when that worked, I tried lifting the foot up and down. It hurt like hell, but it moved the way it was supposed to, so I held out hope that maybe the ankle was badly sprained instead of broken.

"Please say something," he begged. "Can you hear me? Are you okay?"

"I think so," I managed to squeak out with what little air my lungs held now that my diaphragm had started working again.

"Oh, thank God."

I couldn't stand the pain in my right arm any longer, so I pushed up with my left and eased it out from under me.

As the blood flow rushed back into it, a barrage of pins and needles assaulted me. Bracing for more severe pain, I flexed my fingers in and out of a fist and then bent and extended my elbow, but to my surprise, it didn't hurt beyond soreness from the fall. Nothing seemed to be broken. Not with any kind of debilitating fracture anyway.

"Don't move around too much," Brick cautioned. "You're right on the edge."

I already knew that, but his words somehow made it even more terrifying. It felt way too vulnerable to be lying there so precariously, unable to see what was happening around me.

As soon as I felt like my right hand could take the pressure, I slowly pushed up and back into a kneeling position, taking care to stay within the same space my body already occupied.

My stomach flipped when I saw how very narrow the ledge actually was and how close I'd come to plunging all the way to the bottom of the valley and an almost certain death. If I'd gone over the bluff a few feet farther in either direction, I would have missed the ledge completely.

"It's going to be okay," Brick said, his reassurance ringing hollow in light of reality. "I'm gonna get you out of this. I'm gonna get you home."

His words reminded me of the reason for my mad rush through the woods, and I turned, frantically searching the sky for any sign of the tiny lights. It was only then that I noticed how silent the night was, and what that meant.

"Where is the helicopter?"

"They've gone." Brick's voice sounded as dejected as I felt.

"What? Why? Why did they give up so easily?"

"First of all, we don't even know that they were looking for us. It could have been a random helicopter that just happened to be in the area. Don't worry. They're gonna come for us. They will. There's no way they won't find us. But right now, we need to get you off that ledge. I have an idea. Hold on."

"Like I have a choice? Where am I gonna go?"

I had a brief moment of panic when he disappeared, but the sound of his footsteps tromping around and the choice curse words peppering the night air reassured me that he hadn't gone far.

"Here," he said when he returned. "See if you can reach this."

I looked toward his voice at the top of the bluff but was unable to see his face behind the thin, narrow sapling he held extended toward me.

"What the hell? Did you literally pull a tree out of the ground?"

"No. I broke it off near the ground. I needed something long enough to reach you, strong enough to hold you, and light enough for me to maneuver and grip. See if you can grab onto it."

"This is your plan?" I asked as I stared up at the sapling. "You're going to, what? Drag me up the side of the mountain holding onto a thin tree you could snap with your bare hands? What if I can't hold on? What if it breaks? What if you drop me?"

"I won't drop you, and it won't break without someone as big as me kicking the hell out of it and standing on it first. And there's no way someone as tenacious as you is gonna let go. C'mon. See if you can reach it."

"There has to be a better way."

He sighed, resting the sapling against the cliffside. "I'm sure the heroes in your romance books would have plenty of rope on hand and be able to fashion a harness for you. They'd probably even have a horse waiting nearby who could pull you up all leisurely-like, but I'm a bit limited on supplies at the moment. This was the best I could come up with, but hey, if you have a plan, I'm all ears."

"No, I don't, and I wasn't saying—look, I appreciate what you're trying to do, Brick. I just don't want to die, that's all."

"I'm not going to let you die. I've already told you that."

"Yeah, and I've told you that you need to stop saying that since you don't have any control over it."

I pressed my hands to the ground and stood, taking care not to put much weight on my right foot.

"Be careful," he said. "Stay as far away from the edge as possible. The ground may not be stable. There may be loose stones."

Once again, his words made the situation even worse, and I made the mistake of looking beyond the rock beneath me to the trees down below.

I froze.

One wrong step. One stumble. That was all it would take to send me to my death.

"You okay?" Brick asked.

"I'm fine. I just need a minute."

I closed my eyes and drew in the deepest breath I could manage, trying to center my thoughts in an effort to calm my nerves. They refused to be calm, so I switched mind games and focused instead on psyching myself up for the task ahead.

After shaking my hands at my sides with a couple of quick, forceful exhales, I took a step toward the sapling, determined to conquer it. The first hobble-shuffle on my right foot was painful, but it held. The second time I put weight on it, it gave way with a searing pain that made the whole world swim and brought me to my knees with an anguished yowl.

Brick screamed my name as I scooted backward to press against the solidity of the mountainside, getting as far from the edge as space allowed.

Waves of nausea rolled over me as I straightened out my throbbing leg, and I gripped my hand over my stomach, pleading with my body to play nice. The last thing I needed was to vomit on top of everything else I was dealing with.

"What happened?" Brick asked, panicked once more. "Are you all right?"

I was concentrating so hard on not throwing up or passing out that I couldn't spare any energy to answer him, and the lack of a response ramped up the anxiety in his voice even higher.

"Lauryn, what's going on? I'm about to come down there if you don't say something. Answer me. Are you okay?"

"No. Yes. Sort of. I don't know. I'm really woozy," I said with my eyes clenched shut.

"Then sit still," he commanded. "Don't you dare pass out on me."

"It would only be fair, you know, considering you blacked out at the worst possible time earlier."

"Yeah, well, that was out of my control."

As the intensity of the pain in my ankle began to subside, my dizziness and nausea waned, but I stayed pressed against the bluff with my eyes closed, worried that if I moved I'd get hit with another wave.

"How are you feeling?" he asked after a while.

"Less woozy, but I think maybe my ankle's broken. I can't put any weight on it."

He swore loudly. "Those damned heels. I never should have let you leave the crash site. You had no business walking around the woods in the dark in those shoes."

I leaned to the side to glare up at him. "Excuse me? Did you say you shouldn't have *let me leave*? You didn't *let* me do anything. You have no say-so over me. I can go anywhere I damned well please in whatever shoes I want."

"Yes, you can, but common sense says you shouldn't hike in heels."

"I didn't plan on hiking when I put them on!"

"Okay, look, arguing over this isn't getting us anywhere. The situation is what it is, and we need to get you off that ledge and back up here so you can get medical attention when they come. If I could figure out a way to come down and get you, I swear I would, but for right now, this is the best plan we've got. Do you think you can stand up at all? Can you reach this?"

He had extended the sapling toward me again.

Cursing him beneath my breath, I rolled to my knees, which were skinned and bloody and none too happy. Using the rock face for stability, I managed to make it to standing.

My right ankle pulsed with pain, but as long as I didn't put any weight on that foot, the agony was bearable.

Looking up at the sapling, I swallowed hard, hoping to suppress my fears.

"Okay, Lauryn, no one ever accomplished anything without trying. Just do what you can, the best you can," I whispered softly to myself, hearing my mother's voice in my head as I repeated words she'd said to me so many times throughout my life.

Reaching for the sapling, I stretched as far as I could, but my fingertips barely grazed the lowest leaves. The trunk—the only part of the young tree that would possibly hold me—was out of my reach.

"Can you drop it any lower?" I asked.

"Not if I'm gonna have enough leverage to pull you up. I've already a good portion of my upper body hanging over the side as it is."

I tried again to reach it, standing on tiptoes as best as I could with only one foot in play, but it was no use. We were about eighteen inches from connecting. If I'd had both feet, I might have been able to jump for it, but I didn't dare risk landing wrong or falling.

"I can't, Brick. I can't reach it."

"Is there any way you can climb up far enough to reach it?"

"You're kidding, right? I suck at rock climbing when I'm in a facility where they have toeholds and harnesses, and you expect me to do a free climb up the side of a mountain with a broken ankle? I appreciate your confidence in me, but yeah, no."

"All right. Hold on. I have another idea."

He disappeared but was back within minutes. "Can you reach this?"

The blanket was tied like a sling on the end of the sapling, and it dangled just above my head, easily within reach.

"Yeah, I can reach it, but what am I supposed to do with it?"

Brick frowned. "I was thinking you could put your arms through it and hold on, and then I'll pull you up."

I stared at the blanket, terrified to consider what he was suggesting. "What if the blanket comes loose?"

"It won't. I'm confident in my knots."

"Glad one of us is. What if you drop me?"

"I won't."

We stared at each other, but my pain and fear overrode the jolt I'd grown accustomed to feeling when I looked at him.

I wanted to trust him. I wanted to be out of this situation. But there were so many ways for his plan to go wrong.

As I hesitated, trying to summon the courage to make another attempt, something compelled me to look up and to the right.

Perhaps it was some innate instinct that told me I was being watched, or maybe a sound or movement drew my attention without me consciously perceiving it.

There among the foliage farther down the bank of the bluff, Kirby stood looking down at me.

"Kirby!" I yelled up to Brick as I pointed. "It's Kirby!"

Kirby disappeared into the woods as soon as I called his name, and I looked to Brick in a panic.

"He's getting away! He's running. He's right there. Go! What are you doing?"

Brick hadn't moved. He was still lying on his stomach, extending the sapling to me as his eyes held mine. "I don't give a damn about Kirby. All I care about is getting you to safety. Now, put your arms through the sling and hold on tight."

I stared at the blanket, and then as if I'd learned nothing from the last time I did it, I made the mistake of looking behind me towards the bottom of the valley again. It was so far down. So impossibly far. And the ledge was too narrow to take any chances.

"Let's just wait until the rescue crew comes," I said, panic rising in my chest. "They might have one of those basket things, right? They could pick me up in one of those, couldn't they? That would be safer."

"Lauryn, look at me. Listen to me. I am not going to drop you. I will not let anything happen to you, okay?"

"There you go, talking stupid again." My voice crackled with the fear that had tightened my damaged throat. "No one can tell anyone that and mean it."

"I mean it. Grab the blanket. If you're not comfortable using it as a sling, then twist your arms in it and use it to shimmy up to the trunk so you'll have something more stable to hold onto."

Biting down on my lip, I stared up at him.

I just wanted to be home, safe in my bed. I wanted my parents. I wanted to wake up from this terrible nightmare, call Piper, and tell her that she wasn't going to believe what I had dreamed.

Well, maybe I'd call Dani instead of Piper. Piper was insanely terrified of flying already. I couldn't imagine how she must have reacted when they told her my plane had gone down.

I had to survive this. I had to come home. And I damned sure wasn't going to be one of three people out of the whole plane to make it through the crash only to slip off the side of the mountain and fall to my death.

Bracing one hand against the rock face in front of me, I reached up and grabbed the blanket, hooking my arm through it. Then I reached up with the other arm and did the same, tugging to see if his knots would hold.

"Ready?" he asked.

I exhaled slowly, unable to believe I was actually going to attempt this. "As ready as I'm ever gonna be."

He pulled just enough to tighten the sling around my upper back and underneath my arms, and then he lifted me off the ground a couple of inches and stopped.

"You good?" he asked as he held me steady.

"Yeah. You?"

"I'm fine. See if you can use the blanket to climb higher to get a hold on the tree trunk."

Holding the blanket tightly fist over fist, I did as he told me, using my knee against the rock as I climbed to help support my weight and give me leverage so I didn't start swinging.

Once I'd grasped the narrow trunk in both hands, I settled my upper back against the sling. It was wound beneath my armpits and over my arms, and I could only hope that if my hands failed to hold me, the sling would.

"Okay. Let's do this," I said with a sharp exhale as I looked up at Brick. "Don't drop me!"

"I won't. I promise, and you know I always keep my promises."

THIRTEEN

My journey up the bluff was slow and arduous. My already-bloody knees scraped against the rock face several times, and my arms and shoulders ached from holding the weight of my body.

I could only imagine how difficult it must be for Brick to bring me up as basically dead weight, but he never let on that it was a struggle. His voice remained calm and steady as he spoke encouraging words and continued to pull me with relentless determination.

As I neared the top, a breeze blew through, carrying strands of hair across my face and lifting my skirt. Gooseflesh spread across my bare legs as they dangled, but despite the cool air, sweat had beaded across my brow with the physical exertion of holding on, and my hands—numb from the strain of holding the trunk so tightly—had become slippery with perspiration.

My grip began to fail.

"Brick! My hands are sliding."

"Just a little farther. Hold on a little longer, and I'll be able to reach you." His voice had begun to show a bit of tension, and the veins in his arms bulged with the effort of hoisting me. "Don't worry. The sling will hold you."

"What if it doesn't? I'm scared," I shrieked. "I'm slipping!"

He stopped pulling right away and tucked the sapling between his arm and his side, his bicep fully contracted as he wedged the tree between it and his ribs. Then with the other hand, he reached for me. "Take my hand."

"I...can't. If I let go, I'll fall."

My hands slid further, the rough bark stinging my tender palms.

"Brick," I gasped.

"It's okay, Lauryn. You can do it." He stretched his palm farther toward me. "Take my hand."

I don't know why I seemed to be a sucker for terrorizing myself, but in that moment, I looked down. I think maybe I wanted to reassure myself that if I fell, I'd only land on the narrow ledge again, but seeing beyond that ledge to the open air waiting to swallow me only served to drive my panic level into high gear.

"I don't want to die," I said for the second time since we'd met.

"You're not going to. Don't look down there. Look at me. Keep your eyes on me and take my hand."

"If I let go, I'm gonna fall."

"Not if you grab hold of me. Look at me. Lauryn, look at me."

I forced myself to look away from the ground and up at him. The intensity of his stare held me captive, but I still couldn't make myself let go.

My hands slid again, and this time the tree moved a little with me. Brick clamped his arm down on the tree harder, his face taut and his neck corded by the strain it took to hold it.

"Lauryn, now! You have to trust me."

"I can't." My throat felt as though it were closing, and I swallowed hard, fighting the almost unbearable urge to cough. A coughing fit in that moment would surely seal my fate.

"Yes, you can," he whispered. "Please. Trust me. Take my hand."

"I'm scared, Brick."

"I know. I am too, but I won't let you fall. I swear. I've got you, but I can't hold this tree like this forever. Now take my damned hand."

The moment between letting go of the wood and grasping Brick's hand lasted less than a second, but it felt like an eternity.

Then, he had me, just like he said he would.

His hand closed over mine with a vice-like grip, and as he hefted me upward with a powerful jerk, he released the tree, and his other hand clamped around my wrist.

With a couple more tugs, he pulled me up over the side and fell backward with our momentum, carrying me with him onto his chest.

My knees stung, my arm and shoulder ached as though they'd been disconnected at the socket, and my ankle throbbed, but none of it mattered.

Brick's hands were in my hair, and his mouth had claimed mine with an urgency that told me his calmness before had been a facade. He devoured me as though he were a man dying of thirst, and only the taste of me could quench it.

Overwhelmed with relief and elation and overcome by pent-up passion, I met his intensity level full-on, my tongue roiling with his as I gripped his shoulders and moved to straddle his hips.

Suddenly, he tore his lips from mine and held my face in his hands, pulling me back so he could look at me. "Are you all right?"

I nodded and returned my lips to his, craving more. At first, he picked up where we'd left off, just as eager and hungry as before. But then with a groan deep in his throat, he pulled away. Gently rolling me off him and onto my back, he laid his arm over his forehead and closed his eyes.

"I'm sorry," he whispered.

I shifted to lie on my side next to him, propping up on my elbow. "For what? What's wrong?"

"I let it happen again. I don't know what's gotten into me. It's not like me to lose control of my emotions that way. I just...you know what, it doesn't matter. I totally crossed a line, and I shouldn't have. I apologize."

"For what? Uh, in case you didn't notice, I was a more-than-willing participant. I'm sorry if you couldn't tell I was enjoying myself. I'll try to do a better job of conveying that next time."

He frowned and turned his head away, but I laid my hand on his cheek and turned his face back to mine.

"Hey. Brick. You have nothing to feel bad for. I wanted you to kiss me again. You were the one who shut it down before, not me. But I have to ask, if you don't want to kiss me, why do you keep doing it?"

He reached to take my hand from his face and clasped it to his chest. "Lauryn, it's not that I don't want to kiss you. Hell, I've wanted to kiss you since the first time I laid eyes on you."

"You're not the only one. I felt the same way when I saw you the first time. So, why do you keep pulling away?"

"I told you before. I shouldn't do this. I shouldn't let my guard down like this. It's just that when I saw you go over that cliff...when I thought I'd lost you..." He released my hand and rubbed his fingers over his face with a heavy sigh. "I don't even know what I'm saying. Never mind."

"No, please," I pressed my hand against his chest. "Continue. What were you going to say?"

He stared up at me, his eyes darting back and forth as they tracked mine.

"It's crazy," he whispered, "but I feel so close to you. Like we know each other. Like I've known you for a long time."

My heart skipped a beat, and I grinned, biting down on my lip as I weighed how vulnerable I was willing to be in return. "I feel it too. I've never felt anything like this before. This...*connection*...we have."

He reached to caress my cheek, and I leaned in closer, pressing my lips to his for a quick kiss.

I'd intended to plant it and pull away, but Brick grabbed the back of my head and kept me there with our lips joined and still. Though neither of us moved at all, it was one of the most sensual kisses I'd ever experienced.

I inhaled deeply to breathe him in, my entire body aching with the most intense need I'd ever felt. Never had I yearned so fervently for someone's touch, and the flames of desire I'd felt before were merely sparks compared to the roaring inferno blazing inside me.

Longing to taste him again, I brushed my tongue across his lips, and he obliged the request and let me in. Our explorations were much less frantic than before, and somehow, the tenderness proved even hotter than the wild abandon.

It didn't take long for the pace to pick up again though, and as our kiss intensified and our hands began to roam, Brick rose up to push me onto my back. His mouth ravaged mine as he trailed his fingers down my arm, leaving a scorching path of sensations in his wake. He moved his grip to my waist, lingering there as he pulled me against him, and then he slid his hand along the curve of my hip and began to caress the bare skin of my thigh. I shivered beneath his touch, my skin prickling in gooseflesh.

He did break our kiss then, but before I could protest, he had buried his mouth in my neck, his tongue lapping against the hollow of my collarbone. I writhed beneath him, certain his goal was to drive me mad. His tongue burned me like a brand as he suckled his way up my neck to the sensitive area behind my ear, and when he darted his tongue against my ear lobe, I sunk my hands into the hair at the nape of his neck, tilting my head to the side to give him easier access.

Teasing his fingers higher up my thigh, he nudged his hand underneath the hem of my skirt. Desperate for even more contact, I shifted to bend my knee over his leg and pull him closer, forgetting my injury in the oblivion of pleasure. My ankle bumped against the back of his leg, and I yelped with a full-body flinch.

Brick rolled from me immediately, and I sat up, reaching for my ankle.

"Damn, it's pretty swollen," he said. "We should get that shoe off before the strap gets too tight."

He moved to kneel at my feet, placing his hand beneath my calf to lift my foot and place it on his thigh.

I flinched again as he tugged on the strap to thread it back out of the buckle, and he looked up at me with alarm.

"Did I hurt you? I'm trying to be as gentle as I can."

"I appreciate that. I must say, for such a muscular man, you do have a surprisingly gentle touch, but I'm fine. You don't have to be gentle with me."

He lifted an eyebrow at my double entendre, and I grinned with a wink.

Grinning back, he eased the unbuckled shoe from my foot and set it on the ground. "I'm going to resist the temptation to respond and leave that one alone."

"Oh, no, please. Go ahead and say it. I threw the gauntlet; you have to pick it up and meet the challenge."

"I have a feeling if I tried to meet every challenge you offer, I'd be perpetually exhausted. Do you want me to take the other shoe off so you're not lopsided?"

"I'm going to be lopsided either way, but I suppose if I have to hobble, it might be easier to do it barefooted at this point."

Brick frowned. "I don't think you'll be putting weight on that foot any time soon. If you go anywhere, you'll be riding on my back to get there."

As he gingerly set my injured foot back on the ground and then leaned to undo my other shoe, I couldn't help but imagine what it might be like for him to undress me. My mind played it out like a soft-focus film, so realistic I could almost feel his touch on my skin, even in areas his fingers hadn't been...yet.

When he'd gotten that shoe off, he reached to place it with the other one, and I rubbed my left foot along his thigh, creeping it higher as he lifted his eyes to mine.

This time when our eyes locked and the jolt hit me, I had no doubt he felt it too. It pulsed between us like a magnetic field, and we both leaned forward, drawn together by a pull too strong to resist.

"This is madness," he growled, his voice so deep and so low I almost couldn't make out his words. "What the hell are you doing to me?"

He wrapped his arms around me, and when he closed his mouth over mine, any semblance of gentleness or restraint had disappeared. The energy between us exploded in a frenzy, and the stress and tension of the night only served to heighten our need for release.

We clung to each other, unable to get close enough, though I'd pressed my body so tightly against his that it seemed we'd fused into one being. I'd never been kissed so thoroughly that it felt like a sexual experience in and of itself, and when he twisted his tongue around mine to suck it into his mouth, I felt like he was pulling my very soul inside him.

I tugged at his shirt to pull it free from his waistband and then ran my hands beneath it, raking my fingernails up and down his back as a deep groan rumbled in his throat.

He sank his teeth softly into my neck and tugged as I pulled his shirt up to remove it so I could have free rein with his bare skin.

Nudging his knee between my legs, he eased me down onto my back, his lips never leaving my skin. Then, straddling my knee, he raised up and pulled his shirt over his head, exposing the most perfectly sculpted abs I'd ever seen. Possibly the most perfectly sculpted abs *anyone* had ever seen.

I reached to drag my fingernails across the washboard before he could lay back down, and his stomach quivered beneath my touch. Emboldened, I traced a slow circle around his navel and then dipped my finger inside the waist band of his jeans, drawing a line slowly from the deep pelvic groove on one hip over to the other.

His body shuddered as I hooked my fingers lower inside the denim and trailed them back to the point below his navel where a line of soft hair led into his jeans.

Eager to see more of his perfection, I tugged at his belt and began to unfasten it, but he moved his hand over mine and stilled it. Then with a quiet swear, he pushed my hand aside and stood, yanking his shirt back on as he walked a few steps away to stand staring out into the woods with his hands on his head.

FOURTEEN

"What's wrong?" I asked, breathless and confused.

He swore again, more forcefully this time, and then he began to pace back and forth. "I must be losing my mind. I'm so sorry, but I can't do this. We can't do this."

"What do you mean?" My pulse was still pumping at maximum capacity, and every nerve in my body was firing on high alert with the expectation of impending ecstasy, so his sudden shift in gears felt like a bucket of cold water had been doused over me. "Why? What's wrong?"

Looking over his shoulder at me, he frowned. "This. This is wrong. Lauryn, you deserve so much more. So much better. This whole ordeal since I met you has been surreal. It's like we're functioning in some alternate reality, but the decisions we make here will still have real-world consequences. Just because we're removed from our ordinary lives right now doesn't mean we can just do whatever we want with reckless abandon."

His point hit me like another bucket of cold water.

What the hell had I been thinking? What was I doing? Was I really about to have unprotected sex with a total stranger in the middle of the woods?

Yes, I realized with some measure of horror. If Brick hadn't stopped me, I would have. I would have gone through with it blindly and wholeheartedly.

In fact, whether we should or shouldn't hadn't crossed my mind. Somewhere between waking up in the midst of fiery death and dangling by a tree off a mountainside, I had tossed aside my usual reservations and precautions.

I suppose I'd been in survival mode, acting on impulse and so far removed from reality that I'd somehow set aside any thoughts of STIs or pregnancies, as though those didn't exist during near-death encounters. In the vortex of adrenaline I'd been swirling in and the excitement of finding out soulmates might exist after all, I'd somehow thrown reality and caution to the wind and decided to seize the moment along with whatever opportunities it presented.

"Hey, look, I'm sorry," he said, coming to kneel beside me. "The last thing I ever want to do is hurt you. I never expected to meet you, and then when I did...I just need you to know that it's not because I don't want to be with you. I do. But I can't. I can't do that to you."

I shook my head. "No, I totally get it. You're right. We weren't thinking clearly, or at least I know I wasn't. You appeared to be, and thanks for that, by the way. Just so you know, I'm not the type who usually does that sort of thing. I mean, I do *that*. I just meant like, I don't do it with strangers. Not that I'm saying you're a stranger. Well, you are, but, I mean, oh God, could I be any more awkward?"

I covered my face in my hands, and he pulled them away and held them, staring down at our intertwined fingers.

Since I seemed unable to form coherent sentences, I didn't attempt to speak again, but it didn't take long for his silence to become unbearable.

"What are you thinking?" I asked, wishing I could see inside his head.

He didn't respond right away or even acknowledge that I'd

spoken. I thought perhaps he wasn't going to answer, but then he looked up at me and attempted a smile.

"What am I thinking…I'm thinking you are the most incredible, frustrating, interesting, enticing, and infuriating woman I've ever encountered."

"Wow." Blood rushed to my cheeks, and I flushed hot with embarrassment. "That's a lot of adjectives, and not all of them were positive."

He smiled. "I forgot to add courageous, irresistible, and beautiful."

"What about awkward? You gotta throw awkward in there."

"Adorably awkward. I'm sure there are many more that apply, but my head's a little muddled right now and I can't think straight."

"Muddled?" I frowned as I pulled my hand from his and reached to check his bandage. With everything else that was going on, I'd almost forgotten he was injured. "Are you dizzy again? Any nausea? Pain?"

He brushed my hand away and squeezed it. "All of the above, but that's not what has me flustered."

Guessing at what he meant, I grinned as another rush of warmth filled me. "Oh, really? Do tell. What on earth has you flustered?"

He brought my hand to his lips, turning it to place a kiss inside my palm, and then he held it to his chest as his eyes searched mine. "Something unexpected I never thought I'd find, and now that I have, everything I thought I knew makes no sense."

The tenderness in his voice tugged at my heart, but I wasn't sure what to say in response to that. Not wanting to endure another awkward silence, I opted to go with the first thing that popped into my head.

"I think I forgot to say thank you. For the pull-up. You saved my life. Again."

He smiled as he released my hands and shifted from kneeling to sitting. "As long as you stayed put, you would have been fine on the ledge until help arrived. You weren't in any immediate danger, so I hardly think I saved your life by pulling you up. In fact, I may have put you in more danger."

"Oh, yeah? Then why didn't you leave me down there? Why the urgency in bringing me up?"

Leaning back with his hands braced on the ground to support him as he stretched his legs out in front of him, he stared up at the trees above us. "I don't know. I don't know how to explain it. How to explain any of this. I just needed to have you with me. To see for myself that you were okay."

"Well, other than a busted ankle and more bruises and scrapes than I can count, I'm okay."

"So you are."

I leaned forward, laying my hand on his knee, and his eyes returned to mine.

"Tell me your name," I said with a grin.

"Oh, no. This again?" He rolled his eyes and chuckled. "Why do you want to know so badly?"

"Honestly?"

"Of course."

I bit down on my lip, trying to decide how much of the truth to admit. "Because I want to feel special. I want to know something about you that you don't tell other people."

He cocked his head, and his smile faded as the seriousness returned to his eyes.

"Michael," he said softly.

"Really?" I grinned and clasped my hands together, delighted that he'd shared it with me. "That's so normal! Why would you hide that your name is Michael?"

"I'm not hiding anything. I just prefer to go by Brick."

"But why?"

"Why can't knowing my name be enough?"

"Because I want to know *you*, not just your name."

He sighed as he took my hand from his leg and pressed our palms and fingers together, holding them up for comparison. Then he threaded our fingers together and laid our hands back on his thigh.

"I'm a junior. I was named after my father. He died when I was eight."

"Oh, Brick. I'm sorry."

"Me, too. My dad was my hero. He was strong and smart. He never knew a stranger. He had the heartiest laugh. And he loved my mom and me more than anything in the world."

"How did he...what happened? If you don't mind my asking."

"Heart attack. Out of the blue. He was a runner. Ate lean, ran every evening before dinner. Healthy as a horse. Or so he thought. And then one day, he was driving a forklift at work, and he just slumped over the controls. Gone in seconds."

"That's awful. I don't know what to say."

"There's nothing to say. Fate can be cruel."

We both sat silently with our thoughts for a moment as Brick drew circles on the back of my hand with his thumb.

My curiosity became too much to contain, and I had to ask. "Why don't you want to use his name? Is it just too painful?"

"Something like that."

"I think it would be a beautiful tribute to him for you to use his name. Like you're carrying on his legacy."

He dropped my hand and rose to stand, running his hand across his head and then wincing as he touched the bandage.

I sat up, alarmed that I had said something to upset him. "I shouldn't have said that. I shouldn't have said anything. I didn't mean to pry or try to tell you what you should do."

"It's fine. You couldn't know." He sighed and stared down at me. "When my dad died, my mom really struggled. It was hard for her to manage the bills and the house without him, but more than the money, I think she really just couldn't handle him being gone. Being alone. I think having what she had and losing it was too much for her."

A sense of foreboding filled me, and I dreaded what his next words would reveal.

"She hooked up with a guy about a year after Dad died. A real charmer, that one. Paulie. He talked a good game, and he had just enough money to make her think she'd be okay. Once he'd moved in, it all changed. He had a temper that could go from zero to sixty with no warning at all, and fists were the only way he knew to have a conversation. He put her through five years of a painful hell before he put her in intensive care and the grave."

My hand went to my mouth to cover my gasp. I wished I could take back all my questions and keep him from having to revisit his past.

"I'm so sorry, Brick. I never should have pushed you to talk about this."

"No. It's fine." He picked up a dead branch lying on the ground and slung it farther into the woods. "It was a long time ago. Life rolls on. It helps me to remember sometimes. To be reminded of why I do what I do. It keeps me focused on what's important. On my objective. My mission."

"And that's why you go after criminals? It's why you became a cop?"

"Yeah. It is." He looked at me, and I flinched at the cold anger in his eyes. "That piece of shit ran, and no one could find him. So, I bided my time until I turned eighteen, and then I hunted him down and delivered him to the police. I guess the chief saw something in me that he admired, so he took me under his wing and mentored me through the academy. But then I found that I can do a lot more to bring justice if I don't play by the rules."

Tension emanated from him, and I hated that I'd pushed him into the past. Despite the intimacy of what he was sharing, I worried he'd pulled away from me again.

I needed to go to him, to hold him, and somehow bring him back to the present. Back to me.

I rolled onto all fours and then tried to push myself to standing without putting any weight on my right foot.

"What are you doing?" he asked as he rushed to my side, grabbing my elbow to steady me.

"Trying to come to you. I'm sorry. I feel so bad that I brought all this up."

"Don't feel bad," he said, reaching to push a lock of hair behind my ear. His eyes and his voice were tender again, but the tension hadn't left his body. "You didn't force me to talk, Lauryn. I chose to share those things with you, though to be honest, I'm not sure why I did. It's not something I normally do."

The temperature had fallen as the first light of dawn approached, and the air was damp with impending dew. Now that my adrenaline had returned to somewhat normal levels and we weren't moving around as much, the cold seemed to seep into my skin, and I shivered, hugging my arms around me.

"Are you cold?" he asked, wrapping his arms around me. "C'mere."

I buried my face in his chest and wound my arms around his waist, thankful for his warmth and being close again.

I couldn't stop thinking of what he'd revealed about his past. My thoughts turned to Kirby, and what I'd learned about Brick gave me a better understanding of why it was so important to him to bring Kirby back.

"I'm sorry Kirby got away," I whispered. "I hate that I made you break your promise to his mom."

He leaned back and looked down at me. "I'll still catch him. The promise isn't broken yet. I had more important things to attend to at the time. I had a warrior in distress to rescue."

I laughed, which made me cough. A lot. It was a rough spell, and I had to break from his embrace and double over to try and catch my breath.

"Your cough is definitely getting worse," Brick said. "I'm worried about how much residual damage you have from smoke inhalation."

"You seem fine, though. Why would it affect me and not you?"

He shrugged one shoulder. "You exerted yourself with some pretty demanding physical efforts, which requires more oxygen. I was unconscious and taking in the bare minimum air. Besides that, everyone's lung capacities are different anyway. It's why one person can be a life-long smoker and never have an issue, yet another person dies of lung cancer from occasional secondhand smoke."

I coughed again and groaned in agony. My entire body was sore, and with each spasm, I felt every area of pain more intensely.

"Let me get you a water," Brick said. "I dumped everything on the ground over there to use the blanket to reach you."

I watched him walk away with my heart swelling in my chest. How could he mean so much to me in such a short period of time? How could I know so little about him and yet be certain that I was falling in love? I'd never believed in soulmates or fated love, but I had no idea how else to explain the intense attraction and depth of emotion I was experiencing. Unless maybe it was some kind of traumatic emotional response that made me feel bonded to him because of our shared tragedy. But then again, I'd felt the jolt and been attracted before tragedy struck.

FIFTEEN

L ost in my thoughts, distracted and tired, I didn't hear Kirby approaching behind me. I didn't even know he was there until an arm wrapped around my throat and something sharp pressed into my side.

I opened my mouth to scream, but he yanked his arm tighter, which constricted my airway and set me coughing again.

Brick turned and immediately tensed, his hand going to his hip as though he were reaching for the weapon that should have been there.

"Kirby, what the hell are you doing? Let her go."

"I can't. We gonna take a walk," Kirby said, his voice crackling with strain.

Brick took a step toward us, his body rigid but his tone unbelievably casual. "You okay, man? You look a little dazed. Were you injured?"

"Stay back," Kirby cautioned, pulling me tighter against him. "Don't come any closer. Start walking that direction and I'm gonna follow you."

Despite Kirby's instruction, Brick didn't move. "I'm sure you heard the helicopter. They'll probably make another pass soon. We'll get you checked out and make sure you're okay."

"I ain't going back." Kirby's chest heaved up and down against my back, his heart pounding so hard that I could feel it beat.

Brick tucked his thumbs through his belt loops with a grin, and I wondered how on earth he could stand there so calmly when some crazy convict had me in his grip.

"Kirby, you and I talked about this before we ever got on that plane. If you're innocent, like you told me you are, then you need to tell the police the same story you told me."

"You know it ain't gonna matter. They gonna send me back. I violated probation, man, and they ain't gonna let me off just 'cause I blow a whistle."

"You'll have to do some time, yes, but if you go back now, if you tell the truth—"

"I ain't going back." Kirby pressed whatever he held harder into my side, and I looked down to see that it was a jagged piece of glass. He'd taken a piece of fabric from the wreckage and tied it around the glass, binding it to a stick to create a makeshift weapon. I wondered if he'd learned the skill in prison.

"All right," Brick said. "You don't want to go back? You don't have to. I told you when you agreed to come with me that I have no authority to take you in. But I gotta ask, man, what the hell are you doing? How is hurting Lauryn going to help you in any way at all?"

"I gotta do what I gotta do." Kirby shifted his weight from foot to foot, swaying side to side with nervous energy, and I struggled to maintain balance on my left foot as he pulled me back and forth with him. "It's survival. Nothing more. It ain't personal."

"Oh, that's where you're wrong," Brick said, crossing his thick arms as he squared his shoulders back. "If you hurt her, I'm going to take it very personally. So, I suggest you let her go before you make a mistake you can't come back from."

Brick's stance and his tone had grown noticeably more menacing, and Kirby stopped swaying and took a tiny step back, apparently unnerved by the threat. His arm eased up a teensy bit around my throat, but his other hand still held the weapon firmly to my side.

"This is my chance, man. My shot at starting over. It was a freak of fate that we survived that crash. Ain't nobody else did, and no one will be thinking we could've. This is my chance. If the world thinks I'm dead, then I ain't gotta go back to jail."

"Wow," Brick said, nodding slowly with one eyebrow cocked. "That's your plan, huh? You've really thought this through. What about your mom? What will that do to her? Haven't you put her through enough already? She isn't going to take news of your death very well. It will devastate her."

"She's gonna be upset, but she'll get over it. It'll be better than if I was in prison. At least this way, she gets tore up once and moves on. Last time I got sent up, she told me it broke her heart every time she visited and had to leave me behind those walls. This way, I break it once."

"You and I both know Susan would much rather you be alive. Sure, it may break her heart to see you in jail, but I guarantee you she'd rather have that than not see you at all. And you'll get back out eventually."

"No!" Kirby tightened his arm against my neck. "It'll be better this way. Everyone needs to think I'm dead."

"I see a few flaws in your plan, so walk me through it so I understand. How will the authorities think you're dead if they don't recover your body?"

"You didn't see the other half of that plane, man." Kirby shook his head. "There ain't nothing left but ashes. No bodies."

"The part we were in wasn't burnt as badly," I said, hoping if I pointed out the obvious he would see reason. "Our seats were intact."

Brick glared at me with an almost imperceptible shake of his head before his eyes darted back to Kirby.

"I already thought of that," Kirby said. "I got the fire going again. By the time they find our seats, there ain't gonna be nothing left but ashes."

"They can still identify bodies in ashes," Brick said, coming a step closer. "Some things don't burn. They'll know you're not accounted for. And that fire you stoked? It's going to make a great smoke signal to lead them straight to the tail section. You're running out of time to get away, and you're about to run out of chances if you don't release her."

"Why do you need us?" I asked, and Brick glared at me again, his plea for silence obvious, but I was unwilling to remain silent and do nothing while my life was in some desperate man's hands. "Why don't you just run, Kirby? Go! Why are you sticking around here anyway? You could have been long gone by now."

"He can't leave any witnesses to say he survived the crash," Brick said, and as I realized he was right, a new level of fear kicked in.

"We won't say anything," I said, frantic as I tried to turn my head to look up at Kirby. "I swear to you. I'll tell them I was unconscious and I have no idea what happened to you."

Kirby shook his head, seeming more agitated. "It's gotta be this way. I ain't free as long as the two of you know I'm alive."

"C'mon, Kirby. You're not a killer," I pleaded, not knowing if that was true but praying it was. "You tried to help me before. You invited me to come with you. You don't want to kill me."

"She's right," Brick said. "You're not a killer, Kirby. You never have been. You don't have it in you to kill."

It was my turn to glare at Brick. *Really? Why on earth would you goad the man holding me hostage into killing me just to prove he could and would!*

Brick's eyes never left Kirby's. "I, on the other hand, would have no qualms killing you if I had to. And if you hurt her, I *will* kill you. No doubt about it. You need to walk away while you still can."

"I ain't going back to prison. I ain't doing it."

Brick walked forward a few steps, and Kirby retreated, dragging me back with his forearm so tight against my throat I could barely breathe.

"Kirby, let her go. Now." Brick's voice was as hard as cold steel. "I won't tell you again."

"I'm sorry, man. I gotta do this. I gotta be free. You need to start walking. We...we're going back to the plane. To the fire. You walk ahead, and I'll follow you with her. No funny business, or I'll jam this glass so far inside her she'll bleed out before you can do anything to stop me."

Brick dipped his head and then cocked it to the side slowly. His neck cracked with a loud series of pops, and then he twisted his head in the other direction, cracking it again. When he brought it upright again, his icy blue eyes bored through Kirby's with a murderous glare, sending a chill down my spine. He spread his fingers wide by his sides, and then he slowly curled them into fists. He looked almost feral, like he might lunge forward at any second, and I knew when Kirby tensed behind me that he had likely sensed the same thing.

"You won't be free," Brick said, his voice a low growl. "You won't ever be free. You shed one drop of her blood, and I will be on you so fast you won't know what hit you. You won't have time to kill her and still defend yourself against me, and I will tear you apart limb by limb."

Kirby wavered. His grip loosened around my neck, and the weapon came away from my skin enough for me to twist and jam my elbow into his gut with every bit of strength I had left in me. He stumbled back, dragging me with me, but I was able to duck out from under his arm.

Brick slammed into him, knocking Kirby off his feet. The two of them landed on the ground in a tumble of fists and wills.

It didn't last long. With one solid swing from Brick's fist to Kirby's jaw, Kirby's head flew back and his body went slack. Brick rolled him over to pin him facedown with his hands twisted behind him and Brick's knee in his back.

"You okay?" Brick said to me, his eyes sweeping over me as though he were doing his own inventory.

My power move and subsequent escape had required more

weight than my ankle could bear, and I'd collapsed to the ground soon after hurling myself into Kirby. I sat stunned and trembling in an undignified heap with silent tears streaming down my face.

"Yeah. I'm fine." My voice shook, betraying my lie, so I added, "I will be."

Brick pulled the handcuffs from his back pocket and secured Kirby's hands, and then he rose to come to me. He weaved as he walked, shaking his head slightly as though trying to unscramble it, and I knew his dizziness had returned. I hoped he hadn't further injured his head fighting with Kirby.

"Are you all right?" I asked as he knelt beside me.

He didn't answer my question. He just wrapped me in his arms and pressed his lips to the top of my head.

"I'm so sorry, Lauryn."

"For what? Saving my life, yet again?" I pulled away from his embrace, uncomfortable with being confined when my emotions were so raw. Swiping at my tears, I let out a maniacal-sounding laugh at the absurdity of the last twelve hours. "I swear I'm not usually this prone to life-threatening situations. I live a mundane life. Truly, I do. I go to work. I come home. I go to my parents' house for Sunday dinner, and I go for the occasional Saturday morning horseback ride at my cousin's. That's the extent of my exciting life. Oh, and I belong to a trivia league that meets once a week. Other than that, I literally sit home and read or attend online book club chats. This conference I just went to? First time I've flown in years." I motioned to the woods around me. "*This* is not my life. This craziness. This can't be happening to me. I just want to wake up from whatever hellish dream this is."

My tears came faster and harder as I ranted, and by the end of my meltdown summary, I sounded near hysterical. My chest jerked as I drew in ragged breaths and struggled not to outright sob.

Through it all, Brick stared at me, his mouth tight and his brows joined together. He looked like he was in pain, and I was even more certain he must have been injured tussling with Kirby or perhaps he'd made his head injury worse.

When he spoke, his calm and soothing voice was in complete contradiction with the agony on his face. "It's gonna be okay. I'm gonna get you out of here and back to your life. You're gonna have dinner with your parents this Sunday. It might be a while before you climb on a horse by yourself again, but you're going to be fine, Lauryn. You're going back to that life of yours, and you're gonna be fine."

"I know," I mumbled, and then I made a horribly unladylike snorting sound as I tried to manage the barrage of snot my hysteria had produced. Sitting up straighter to square my shoulders, I wiped my nose on my sleeve in equally unladylike fashion, and then I exhaled with a loud huff. "I know I'll be fine. It just all became a little much to process for a moment, and I had to get it out. I'm good now." I nodded to reassure both of us. "I'm all right, I swear. But I'm worried about you. About your head. Are you okay?"

"Yeah," he said, much less convincing than I had been, which wasn't much. "I want to get you back to the tail section."

"What about him?" I asked, glancing toward Kirby, who had begun to rouse.

"He's not going anywhere until I get ready to take him somewhere."

"But is he gonna be okay? What's gonna happen to him?"

"Let me worry about Kirby. He never should have been your problem."

"You won't, um, like, uh,— "

"No, Lauryn, I won't hurt him, if that's what you're asking. I would have, if he'd harmed you, but he's restrained now, and I don't go around beating up defenseless men. My first priority is to get you to safety, and once I do that, I'll make sure Kirby is taken into custody and flown back to Florida with the proper authorities. I'll do all I can to help Susan get a chance to speak to him, but his actions tonight prove that he can't be trusted to do the right thing on his own."

Brick's demeanor was eerily subdued. He felt distant, like a wall had been built between us.

I wished I'd let him hold me before when he'd tried. I'd been too antsy then to be comforted. I'd felt like I was coming out of my skin and needed space. But now, I wanted nothing more than to be back in his arms.

"You sure you're all right?" I asked, wondering how he would react if I reached for him, but scared of how much it would hurt if he rejected the offer as I suspected he would.

"I'm fine." He stood upright and laid his hand on a tree trunk to steady himself, and then he looked back at me but didn't make eye contact. "I'm gonna carry you back to the plane."

I opened my mouth to protest, but then shut it as reality set in. My feet were bare, and I was unable to walk on my own. Even if the wreckage had been close—and it wasn't—I'd be hard-pressed to hobble through the woods without injuring myself further. There was a time for independence and determination, and there was a time to admit defeat and accept help. This was the latter.

But I was also uncertain he'd be able to carry me such a distance in his present condition. He was injured too, and obviously struggling.

"You don't have to *carry* me. Maybe I could just lean on you like a crutch. Maybe we could lean on each other."

He cocked one eyebrow and looked down at my foot, which had swollen to a grotesque size and had begun to turn what appeared to be blue in the dawn's increasing light.

"Add stubborn to that list of adjectives," he said. "It would be so much easier for us both if you'd just let me carry you."

"How is that easier for you? You lifted me up a mountainside already; you know that even though I'm short, I'm solid! With the way you're wobbling, I know you're still dizzy and nauseous. It isn't going to help either of us if you fall while you're carrying me. Then, we're both screwed."

"I won't fall. I'm fine." He moved closer and then turned his back to me and did a half-squat. "Lean forward against me, and I'll reach back and lift you up. Can you do that without it hurting you too much?"

"I can do it, but I'm—I—there's got to be another solution. Why don't we stay here, and then when we hear the helicopter come back, we can signal them?"

Straightening with a sigh, he shook his head. "Our best chances of being seen are if we're in that small clearing with the fuselage. And if Kirby lit that fire like he said he did, then the smoke will be a beacon to lead them to us. Is there any way you could just not fight me on this? I'd been up for thirty-six hours straight when I got on that plane, and granted, I've gotten more sleep than you have since I was knocked out cold for a few hours, but I'm exhausted, and I'm sure you are, too. I don't want to argue with you, Lauryn. I just want you to be safe and well, and this is the best way I know to try and achieve that."

SIXTEEN

I'd been fueled by adrenaline for so long that I hadn't thought about being tired, and Brick had been such a machine since regaining consciousness that I hadn't considered his own level of exhaustion. Now that he'd mentioned it, I could see it in the way his eyes had begun to droop and in the deep lines of his forehead and the downward pull of his mouth.

"If you're exhausted, that's all the more reason you shouldn't try to carry me."

"I'm accustomed to functioning when exhausted. Will you please just let me do this for you?"

Something in his plea tugged at me. There was an air of defeat I hadn't sensed in him before, and a sadness in his eyes that made me want to grant whatever wish I could in hopes of taking it away.

"All right. Fine. We'll do it your way," I said, and for a moment, it worked.

The tension in his face softened, and his eyebrows raised in surprise.

"I get the feeling those aren't words you say very often," he said with a grin so damned enticing it made submitting to him worth whatever the cost may be.

I rolled my eyes but couldn't help grinning back at him. "Yeah, well, enjoy them while you can. But if you feel dizzy at all, or if I get too heavy and you need a break, we're stopping. Got it?"

"Yes, ma'am. I got it. Let me check on Kirby and let him know what's going on."

He knelt by the young man, speaking quietly with him. Then the two of them rose, and Brick pulled his belt from his jeans and threaded it through the handcuffs and then around a tree trunk to secure Kirby until he returned.

"Is he all right?" I asked, staring past Brick toward Kirby.

"He's fine."

"You're not going to just leave him there, are you?"

Brick glanced over his shoulder to Kirby and then back to me. "Until I can get you safe and get back here, yes. Are you ready?"

"No, but I don't think I'm ever going to be, so it doesn't matter. How do I do this?"

"First, you need to move your bag to your back," he said, motioning to the small backpack purse on my chest. "Here, hand it to me and I'll put a couple of waters in here in case you have another coughing fit."

Once he'd filled the small bag and I'd pulled it on, he bent and motioned for me to lean across his back. Then, he reached his hand behind him and around my hips to swoop me up and over. I wrapped my arms around his neck as he put his hand beneath my rump to push me higher until I was situated squarely on his back.

Standing upright, he threaded his arms beneath my knees and tugged me closer. "You good?"

"Aye, aye, captain."

We set out through the woods, and I was thankful for the ever-increasing light as day broke. For the first few yards, I worried Brick might stumble and take us down, but he trudged along like a machine once more, as if he didn't even notice the extra weight on his back.

At first, we were both silent. I assumed Brick was focused on the trek, and conscious of the effort he was making both physically and mentally, I remained quiet so as not to tax him further.

But then the maddening silence began to wear on me, and I had to speak.

"How are you feeling? Still dizzy?"

"It's manageable," he said. "And you? You comfortable?"

"I wouldn't say *comfortable*, but I'm good."

In truth, my back ached from trying to hold myself upright so I didn't slump like dead weight against him. The various cuts, bruises, and scrapes all over my body stung and ached, and even though Brick held my right leg a little farther from his body to ensure my foot didn't bump against his thigh, each step he took jarred my ankle and sent pain shooting up my leg.

"You'd be more comfortable if you relaxed, you know. You don't have to be so rigid."

"I'm trying not to weigh you down."

He chuckled and glanced over his shoulder at me. "You do realize you weigh the same no matter how staunchly you sit, right?"

"Well, yes, but I didn't want to just fall all over you. I'd hate for you to regret that you offered."

He gently squeezed my leg and leaned his head back, turning it so he could look at me.

"Trust me, Lauryn. I will never regret having a chance to be close to you."

I smiled and relaxed a little so that my chest rested against his back. Loosening my arms around his shoulders, I leaned forward, nestling my head alongside his.

"Better?" he asked.

"Much," I whispered against his ear. "Thanks."

I wasn't sure how he knew where we were going. The woods all looked the same to me, but he moved ahead without any hesitation, so I had to assume he had some kind of internal GPS leading him back to the crash site.

Without a clear sense of how far we'd come and how far we had to go, I didn't know how to measure whether we were getting close, but when the smell of smoke wafted through the trees, I knew it couldn't be much farther.

As the morning sun brightened the world around me, I grew more confident that we'd survive and be rescued. I'd tried not to give much thought to what would happen between Brick and me once we returned to our normal lives, but now that my thinking had begun to extend beyond immediate life or death, I allowed myself to consider the possibilities.

"Where do you live?" I asked.

"Are you asking what address I have on my driver's license, or where I spend my time?"

"Both, I guess. Are they not the same?"

"I pretty much live on the go. Sometimes that's in my truck. Sometimes it's a cheap motel. Sometimes it's wherever I happen to be when I get a moment to lay down my head. You don't get to plan ahead much when you're tracking someone who doesn't want to be found, so you take what you can get when you get it."

"And you enjoy this lifestyle?"

"I wouldn't say I necessarily *enjoy* it. It is what it is."

"So, how often are you home?" I'd be lying if I said I wasn't already looking ahead to what our dating life might be like and wondering how often I'd get to see him.

"It varies. Some months maybe a couple of nights here and there. Sometimes less. On rare occasions I may get a week or two off, but I've usually already lined up the next job before I finish the current one, so more often than not they're back-to-back."

I frowned as I realized we wouldn't see each other very much at all. "It doesn't sound like your job leaves you much time for a life."

"My job is my life, Lauryn. There's no room for anything else. Or anyone else. That's just the way it is. The way it has to be."

His words stung as though he'd slapped me.

I'd been willing to accept that it would be hard to make things work between us with his schedule as crazy as it was, but his statement made it seem like he didn't even want to try. Like he hadn't even considered it a possibility.

Had what we shared meant nothing to him? Was I completely delusional in thinking we'd both thought this was something special?

He'd said he felt the same connection I did, and based on his behavior after pulling me up the cliff, that seemed to be true.

But then again, he'd pulled away every time things heated up.

While I'd been building white picket fences in my own head, he certainly hadn't made any declarations or promises that indicated he was doing the same.

How could I have been such an idiot? Why on earth had I let my guard down? I couldn't believe I'd bought into the romance propaganda that a chance encounter between strangers could lead to something as ridiculous as fated love.

Brick might have been attracted to me, but he had never intended for us to pursue that connection once we left this mountain, and that realization was like a knife to my already stressed-out heart.

This had been without any doubt the absolute worst night of my life, and the only silver lining—the only bright spot that had given me hope—was Brick. After everything that had happened, his rejection was almost more than I could take.

"Put me down, please," I demanded, unable to remain on his back as I struggled to process this new information.

"Why?" He immediately stopped and bent to help me down. "What's wrong?"

I intended to refuse his assistance, but as I began to slide off him in a rather ungraceful manner, he reached back to wrap his arm around my waist and set me gently on the ground before I could protest.

"Are you okay? What's wrong?" Brick asked again, his eyes sweeping over me as though he were searching for the reason I'd stopped him.

"You don't intend to see me again once we leave here, do you?"

He frowned and looked away, placing his hands on his hips.

I felt so many things all at once that my body trembled with the effort to contain it all. Hurt. Disappointment. Embarrassment. Anger, though I had no right to be angry with him. Betrayal, which was unfair since he'd never made any heart-promises to betray. And fear. Fear that I'd never find a connection on this level again. I'd gone twenty-five years without ever meeting someone who made me feel the way Brick did. How was I supposed to just let him go, knowing I may never experience it again?

But what other choice did I have if he didn't feel the same way about me?

I wanted to walk away. I wanted to be alone to nurse my wounded pride and shattered heart. But with my stupid ankle out of commission, I couldn't go anywhere on my own, even if I did know which way to go—which I didn't.

But I wasn't about to climb back on top of him. No way in hell. I felt humiliated by my helplessness, but I'd sit right there on the ground and wait for someone to find me before I depended on him so completely again.

Since I couldn't leave, I just turned my back and crossed my arms, wishing he would just slink away into the woods and leave me to grieve my silly dreams on my own.

"Lauryn, I told you that I couldn't do this. I tried to explain. I thought you understood."

I spun as fast as I could with only one foot to balance me. "Obviously not. I thought I understood that you felt the same connection I did. I thought you felt like you *knew* me," I said with air quotes. "I thought you were going to swallow me whole with your kisses and damned near make me lose my mind with wanting you. But I thought at the time you wanted me just as badly. Clearly, I was wrong."

He rubbed his hands across the top of his head and then locked them behind his neck as he swore. "You weren't wrong. I did feel a connection with you. Do feel, still. And yes, I do feel like I know you. Like I've known you all my life and was just waiting to find you. And

I wanted to swallow you whole and lay you back on the top of that cliff and bury myself inside you to make you mine. Guilty as charged. But none of that changes the fact that I can't allow myself to love someone. I made a commitment to dedicate my life to a mission, and nothing or no one can interfere with that mission."

"Then why say those things to me, Brick? Why kiss me at all or hold me at all if you knew it wouldn't matter?"

He swore as he stared up at the morning sky through the trees, dropping his mouth open and shaking his head.

"I don't know." Looking back down at me, he shrugged one shoulder. "I honestly don't know. I'd never felt for someone what I felt for you. I tried to walk away from you, and I couldn't. I tried to keep my distance, telling myself that I just had to hold it together until we got out of here. But then when I saw you fall, when you went over the edge..." He tucked his bottom lip over his teeth and bit down on it as he stared down at the ground. "In that moment, when I thought you were...gone...I knew nothing else mattered but you."

My heart twisted. I didn't know if hearing him confirm his feelings made me feel better or worse. The end result hadn't changed, after all. No matter what he felt and what he'd sworn to himself then, he'd decided since then that he wasn't going to act on it. He'd rejected me and his feelings.

"Then what changed your mind?" I asked, needing to know even though it would likely make me feel worse.

He leaned back against a tree trunk and braced his hands on his knees, looking even more exhausted than he had before. "It was all moving so fast. I had you in my arms, and I wanted you like I've never wanted anyone or anything. It was all-consuming, and I've never felt that way about anything other than vengeance. Somehow, I knew that if I went through with it, if we sealed our bond that way, then my life would shift. My priorities would change. I've spent almost my entire life dedicated to a cause, Lauryn. I can't just turn my back on that because I met a beautiful girl on a plane."

"No one's asking you to! What the hell? You think I would just tell you to give up your job and the things you're passionate about because we got together? That would be pretty toxic. Who would want to be in that kind of relationship? I certainly wouldn't want you to come sweeping into my life and tell me I had to give up books or stop working at the library. Why would I do that to you?"

"With all due respect," he said with a sigh, "my job would affect our life together far more than the time you spend reading books."

"Yeah, well, with all due respect, you have no idea how much time I spend reading books. Never underestimate the draw of *one more chapter*. But you're not even willing to give us a chance. You didn't even try to make it work. This spark we feel, that doesn't happen to everyone. You know that, right? And yet, you're willing to throw it away without even bothering to see where it might lead."

He closed the distance between us and stared down at me, his brilliant blue eyes bright with emotion. "You don't understand. My life isn't conducive to relationships. How would you feel never knowing where I am or when I'll be back? How long would it take before you got tired of me missing birthdays or holidays or special occasions? What if I can't call for days? What if you have to go months without seeing me? You really think you'd be okay with that? I told you before, and I meant it...you deserve more. So much more. You deserve a man who can be by your side, fully committed to you and only you. And as much as it kills me and as much as I know I will regret it, I can't be that man."

What he said made sense, and it would be self-destructive for me to argue against my own best interests. But my heart couldn't bear the thought of never seeing him again. Of never feeling the jolt between us again. Of never knowing why we felt what we did.

"Why would we have this connection if it means nothing?"

"It means something, Lauryn. I just don't know what. Maybe we were meant to help each other survive this night and nothing more. I don't know." He cocked his head and stared at me with a frown. "Can you please not look at me like that?"

"Like what?" I asked, crossing my arms.

"Like I'm the villain in your story. I don't want you to be angry with me."

Flinging my arms to my sides, I groaned. "I'm not angry with you, Brick. I'm angry with...fate. With life. With whatever supreme being thought this would be a good idea. I get what you're saying, okay? Yeah. You're right. We probably wouldn't work out too well. I just think that sucks, and I'm sorry if I can't put on a happy face about it for you."

"I'm not happy about it either, okay? So much so that I obviously overrode my own mind several times since we met. I even wavered after I told you it wasn't going to work and that you deserved more. But then when that bullshit happened with Kirby, it just solidified what I already knew to be true. I should have heard Kirby coming, but I didn't, because I was distracted by what was happening between us. I should have known where he was and had him detained already, but I was too focused on you."

"Are you actually saying it's my fault I got held hostage by your friend?"

"No, not at all. And he's not my friend. He's a casual acquaintance, at best. What I'm saying is, I'm no good for you, Lauryn. I deal with some pretty messed up people, and more often than not, I make them and their associates angry. A life with me would put you in danger, and I'm not willing to ever again risk someone retaliating against me to hurt you."

"Kirby wasn't retaliating against you. He was trying to get rid of us both because we knew he was alive."

"But Kirby wouldn't have been on that plane if it wasn't for me. He wouldn't have had any reason to harm you if not for me."

"True, because if you hadn't pulled me into that empty seat, I'd still be in my own, and I'd be dead already."

He flinched at my words as I turned from him to cough.

The wind had shifted, and the air around us was becoming increasingly smokier. My lungs protested breathing in the vile toxicity, and my throat, which had never stopped being irritated, started to burn again.

The coughs had moved deeper into my chest and were much more wet than before.

"I don't like the sound of that," Brick said as I took my bag off to take out a water bottle. "It's definitely getting worse. Your voice is changing, too. It's hoarser."

"I think that's from all the coughing," I said between swigs of water. "My throat had eased up a bit before, but now it's getting really sore again."

I drank about half the bottle and then slid the bottle back inside my bag before fishing around the bottom for another of the peppermints.

Brick laid his hand on my forehead after I'd popped the candy into my mouth, and then he frowned again. "You don't seem to have a fever. How are you feeling other than the cough?"

I shrugged as I did a mental inventory. "My head hurts a little, but again, I think that's because I'm coughing so damn much. My lungs are all fired up, but that's because it's getting smokier the closer we get to the—"

Brick held up his hand and made a shh sound.

It took me a moment to zone in on what he had heard.

"It's a helicopter!"

He nodded. "More than one, I think."

Bizarrely, I felt both elated and distraught. If the helicopters had returned and Kirby's fire was still smoking, then they were sure to find the tail section. We only needed to make it there to be rescued.

I'd be able to contact my family. I could go home. To shower and sleep in my own bed and see my mom, dad, brother, and cousins. The arrival of the helicopters meant the end of the nightmare, and for that, I was grateful and relieved.

But their arrival also signaled goodbye between Brick and me. The next few moments with him would be my last, and then he would go back to his life and I'd go back to mine, forever changed by everything that had transpired on this mountain.

"So, then that's it?" My voice cracked with the question, and it was impossible to tell how much of the thickness in my throat was damage from coughing and how much was raw emotion. "We just go our separate ways and never meet again? We pretend none of this ever happened?"

He reached to cup my cheek in his hand, and his eyes seemed to mirror the pain and confusion I felt.

"I don't think either of us would be able to pretend it never happened, Lauryn. I know I couldn't. I wouldn't want to. I don't want to forget one moment I had with you." He leaned forward to press his lips against my forehead, and then he stared at me with tender eyes as his thumb stroked my cheek. "I fear this face will haunt my dreams for the rest of my life."

The lump in my throat grew larger, and my eyes grew glassy with the emotions threatening to overtake me.

Pulling away from Brick, I turned and gazed toward the sky, blinking rapidly to fight back the tears but playing it off as an attempt to search for the approaching helicopters.

They continued to grow louder by the minute. They were coming closer, and there was definitely more than one this time.

"How are we going to signal them in the daylight?" I tried to ask, but when I spoke, my throat gurgled, and something thick and wet came up. Covering my mouth with my hand as I coughed, I looked down to see black streaks of mucus across my palm.

I gasped but was unable to get air. I was choking on the thick sludge in my throat, and at the same time, my lungs felt as though I'd been trapped beneath a wave and they were filling with water.

The last thing I remember was the sound of the blades whirring and Brick screaming my name as the lights went out.

SEVENTEEN

I woke in the hospital with my parents on either side of my bed.

As soon as the intubation tube was removed from my throat, I asked about Brick, but Mom and Dad had no idea who I was talking about.

At my insistence, they contacted the rescue team to inquire about Brick's wellbeing. They were told he had carried me unconscious in his arms to the crash site where he signaled them. He wouldn't agree to be examined himself until after I'd been placed on oxygen and was on my way to the hospital.

They had no further updates on his condition or his whereabouts, and due to legalities, they were unable to give us his contact information.

News reports about the crash mentioned three survivors, but they said our names were being withheld due to an ongoing investigation involving the US Air Marshals.

It was as though Brick no longer existed, and if I didn't have the rescue workers to confirm my story and the news report confirming three survivors, I might have convinced myself the whole ordeal was a delusion brought on by the trauma of the crash.

I learned when I woke that I'd been unconscious for three days, and that I had almost died from lung damage caused by smoke inhalation.

They'd even told my parents not to get their hopes up, but neither Mom nor Dad is the type to give up easily.

And evidently, neither am I. My doctors said I defied the odds and my grandma kept calling me her miracle.

When I was finally discharged, I moved back into my old bedroom at my parents' house, partly so my mother the nurse could have me under medical observation pretty much twenty-four-seven, but also because I wasn't ready to be alone at my apartment just yet.

After initially indulging due to a morbid curiosity, I had to cut myself off from any coverage of the crash or any details about the people who had lost their lives. Two were doctors. One was a scientist working on a cure for Alzheimer's. One was a world champion figure skater destined for the Olympics. Most were parents, and all were, of course, beloved and missed.

Their stories overwhelmed me, and I'd lie awake at night wondering why I'd been spared when they hadn't. Why me, who had so little to offer the planet?

Nightmares plagued me, so I rarely slept through the night. Most of the time, it was the crash and its aftermath that left me screaming in my sleep, but some nights it was a tall stranger with beautiful blue eyes and a mischievous grin that haunted me. I'd wake from both wild-eyed, drenched in sweat, and gutted to my core for completely different reasons.

For the first month, I had this crazy spark of hope that lit up every time the phone rang or any time someone knocked on our door. It was ridiculous, of course. We'd never even exchanged last names, much less phone numbers or addresses. But he was a tracker, so I knew if he wanted to find me, he would.

Eventually, as more time passed with no word from him, I had to accept Brick had meant what he said. There was no room in his life for me, and he'd obviously moved on, so I had no choice but to do the same.

For the second month, I languished as I tried to acclimate myself back to normal and ignore that everything was different. I was uncharacteristically jumpy. Loud noises could make me cry. Riding in a car gave me anxiety. My family walked on eggshells because I was irritable one minute and tearful the next, and even the slightest hint of smoke could derail my health for days.

Based on my mother's concerned research, those all seemed to be acceptable behaviors for someone who had survived such a traumatic near-death event.

But I knew the crash wasn't the only thing affecting me. For the first time in my life, I had no interest in reading. Romances made me bitter. Heroes of any genre pissed me off, and even the slightest hint of a heroine in distress gave me flashbacks.

I told myself it was insanity to miss someone so deeply when I'd only known him a matter of hours, but somehow in that short period of time, he'd branded my heart and claimed my soul as his own. I reasoned that perhaps my mind had bonded the experience of survival with my attachment to him, making it seem much more in depth that it actually was. But attaching a reasonable explanation did nothing to make it hurt less.

By month three, I'd begun to feel a bit better, and though I still struggled with survivor's guilt and finding a purpose to make my being here worthwhile, I was able to immerse myself in work again.

By the time the four-month anniversary of the crash rolled around, I could lose myself in a story as long as it had not even a trace of romance. Or tragedy. Or death.

Needless to say, that left me with limited options in full-length novels.

At the six-month mark, I was able to drive my own car and I had begun to socialize again. Well, to the limited extent that I'd ever socialized. Basically, I accepted invitations to gather with my cousins and other family members.

My nightmares came less frequently, and I was surprised to find that I could sometimes go two or even three days without thinking about the crash.

I looked forward to the day when I could say the same about Brick. Without fail, each day I'd hear something or see something that made think of him. I wondered where he was, what he was doing, and if he ever thought about me. He'd told me he'd regret letting me go and that my face would haunt his dreams. I selfishly hoped that was true.

As I approached seven months past the crash, my life had returned to its routine for the most part. I still couldn't stomach reading romance, so I'd disconnected from my former online chats, but I'd thrown myself into urban fantasy and science fiction, and I'd begun to find new groups to plug into.

One of those groups had scheduled a Friday night chat to discuss a new release, and I'd been looking forward to hearing insight about the book from other readers. I'd even planned to leave the library a little earlier than usual that evening so I'd have plenty of time to make myself dinner and get settled before going online.

Unfortunately, our mayor had hired a freelance grant writer who had then ghosted him, and he'd dumped the task on my desk when I returned from lunch and asked if I could submit the completed grant application by the six o'clock deadline. And by *asked*, I mean he told me it must be done.

I loathe grant writing, which he knew, and to try and pull together the required information and compose a convincing pitch in a matter of hours had stressed me to the point of wanting to pull my hair out.

While I hadn't tugged hard enough yet to remove any strands from my scalp, I'd run my hands through it enough that it was standing on end and quite the tangled mess.

I'd just leaned back in my chair and rubbed my hands over my face when my director, Christine, came walking into the office.

"You have a visitor."

"A *visitor?*" I spun my chair to face her. "Who? Oh, God. Is it a reporter?" My stomach lurched in fear. "Did someone figure out my name?"

She crossed her arms, and it was only then that I realized she was grinning from ear to ear.

"He knows your name, but he's no reporter. He says he needs a recommendation for a romance novel."

Rolling my eyes, I turned back to the computer screen. "Ugh. It's Ted from the meat market, isn't it? I swear he never gives up. No matter how many times I've said no, he thinks if he can come up with some clever way to ask me out, I'll change my mind. Can you tell him I'm busy? Maybe recommend a novel for him?"

"This is most definitely not Ted from the meat market, and I think you probably want to come and see this one yourself." Smirking, she fanned herself. "He. Is. Hot."

That tiny glimmer of hope that I'd try to douse, dampen, and destroy sparked back to life inside me, and I spun my chair back to her with wide eyes.

"What does he look like?"

"Hmm. Like Thor has a twin?"

My heart began to pound, and I flopped back against the chair in shock.

It couldn't be. After all this time with no word? But who else would it be? Why would a stranger ask me to recommend a romance novel? I mean, I worked in a library so recommending books was sort of my thing, but he could have asked Christine more easily. Why request me?

Christine lifted an eyebrow with a cock of her head. "Well? Are you gonna come out or what should I tell him?"

I smoothed my hair as best as I could and tried to breathe normally.

What would I say? How would I act? Why was he here?

He wasn't. He couldn't be.

I started for the office door, but then hesitated. The last thing I wanted was to go bounding out there thinking it was him and feel like I'd been punched in the gut when it wasn't.

"Can you ask his name?"

Christine nodded and disappeared, and I tried not to get my hopes up. It wasn't him. It couldn't be. It wouldn't be. It was probably some husband who had been sent to pick up a book for his wife, and she'd told him to ask for me. But it didn't make sense that Christine wouldn't know him, and no one in our small town looked anything remotely like Thor.

By the time Christine returned, I'd hastily brushed my hair and put on a fresh coat of lip gloss, just in case. Fridays tended to be a bit more casual at the library, so I was wearing a pair of lavender denim capri pants with a white poet's blouse and a pair of pink and lavender striped canvas sneakers. Not exactly the outfit I would have picked had I known I was going to see Brick again.

"He says his name is Michael."

My heart fluttered so fast I felt dizzy, and I grabbed onto the desk with both hands and did a few slow exhales.

"Are you all right?" Christine asked, her smile fading as her eyes filled with concern.

"Yeah. I just feel like I'm gonna faint."

She sprang into action, moving to scoot the chair closer behind me. "Seriously?"

"No. Well, maybe; who knows?"

"You don't have to see this guy. Do you want me to tell him to leave? You could slip out the back."

"Hell no. I've been waiting seven months for this. I'm not going anywhere, and neither is he."

EIGHTEEN

He looked even better than my memories. He'd had a haircut, and he was obviously more well-rested than the last time I'd seen him.

The blue eyes that had haunted me lit up when they saw me, and the smile I could never forget spread wider than I'd ever seen it.

The jolt was every bit as powerful as it had been the first time I saw him, and not even my heartache could dampen its intensity.

As I walked toward him, he put his hand on his chin and then in his pocket, and then he pulled it from his pocket and ran it across his hair.

I'd never seen him appear nervous, and somehow, it made him even more handsome.

I was nervous, too. My palms felt sweaty, and my stomach seemed to be under siege by an entire legion of butterflies.

My emotions skittered all over the place. Part of me wanted to sprint across the library and jump into his arms like we were in a cheesy rom-com movie. I could even see it play out in my head—my arms around his neck and my legs around his waist as he spun me right there between the *New Release* table and the return desk. My lips even tingled from the imaginary kiss we shared. But another part of me—the cynical part that recalled every single night I'd cried myself to sleep—wasn't willing to jump so quickly into the arms that had rejected me.

He'd dropped off the face of the earth without even checking to see if I'd survived, and I wasn't sure I could forgive him for that, no matter what he had to say.

"Hello, *Michael*," I said, stopping a few feet from him with crossed arms. I forced myself not to smile, even though everything in me was soaring with joy at seeing at him again.

His own grin faded a bit with my frosty reception, but he still seemed so happy to see me that it didn't disappear completely. "Hi. How've you been? God, you look great."

I gave a curt nod, almost trembling with the effort it took not to go to him.

"Thanks. I'm good. What brings you in? Because I'm fairly certain you aren't here for a romance novel recommendation. If so, we have an entire table of recommended reads right over there."

His lips twisted together as though he were trying to contain his smile, his eyes so bright they were almost glowing.

"Yeah, I saw the table, but actually, this is a bit of a special request. A very particular story, and I'm positive you're the only one who can help me find it."

"Oh? Why's that?" I cocked an eyebrow and hoped my outward appearance didn't betray the intense conflict playing out inside me. I was literally tensing every muscle I could in an effort to look calm and stand still despite what felt like high voltage electricity coursing through me.

"Well, you see there's this hero in the story, and he screwed up. Royally. Like, he screwed up bad. He thought he was doing what was best for the heroine. That's what he wanted—for her to be happy. And he thought she'd be happiest if he left the, uh, kingdom." He was talking with his hands, something I hadn't seen him do before, and the fact that he was so nervous felt satisfying somehow. "But the problem is, the hero can't stop thinking about her. She's the first thing he thinks of when he wakes up in the morning and the last thing his mind sees before he goes to sleep at night. He thought he could go back to his life the way it was before her, but it's just not working out for him. Without her, nothing seems the same anymore."

A huge lump formed in my throat, but I swallowed it down, admonishing myself not to give in so easily. Seven months. He'd had seven months to deliver this message. Where had he been all that time if what he was saying was true?

"I think I recognize this story," I said, shifting my weight from one foot to the other. "It's the one where the hero made a very good case for why the heroine was better off without him. It was quite convincing. Why should she think the situation has changed?"

His smile disappeared as he moved toward me. "I'm sorry, Lauryn. I know I screwed up. There's so much I need to tell you. What time do you get off? Could we go somewhere to talk?"

"You're gonna walk in here on a Friday night at five o'clock and assume I have no plans?"

"N-n-no, not at all," he stammered. "I didn't mean to assume that. You had said that you have dinner with your parents on Sunday and do horseback riding on Saturday, so I thought maybe Friday might be a good time, but yeah, you're right. That was very presumptuous of me." His face tensed, and he swallowed hard. "Are you, um, seeing someone?"

"No, not that it would be any of your business if I was."

He released a breath he must have been holding, and his smile returned. "If tonight doesn't work, is there, I don't know, maybe another time that we could talk? Maybe this weekend? I'd love to buy you dinner. Or breakfast. Lunch. Coffee."

I wanted nothing more than to talk to him. I wanted to know where he'd been and what he'd been up to and why he hadn't contacted me before now. But I hated that he had assumed I had no life and no plans for the weekend. He was right, of course, and I hated that too.

I didn't hate it so much that I was willing to send him away though.

"I'm in the middle of something, so I won't be done here for an hour or so."

He smiled with another exhale and a shrug. "I can wait around if that's okay."

"Sure, but we lock up at five."

"Yeah, all right." He pointed toward the door. "I'll just be outside in my truck. Come on out whenever you're done."

Nodding, I rubbed my lips together to keep from smiling as I walked backward away from him. "Right. Okay."

My shoes felt like they were filled with concrete. I didn't want to go. I didn't want to let him out of my sight. I didn't want him to disappear again.

I backed into a display of paranormal mysteries, and after straightening it, I began to walk away but then paused and turned back.

"What's your last name?"

His brows twitched together briefly as though he were curious or confused. "Hendriks."

"Michael Hendriks," I said, and he nodded.

"Junior. Michael Hendriks, Junior."

I wondered why he was now identifying himself with his given name instead of his nickname, and I made a mental note to add that to the questions I wanted answers for.

When I'd reached the hallway that led to the office, I paused with my hand on the corner of the wall and looked over my shoulder. He stood where I'd left him, still grinning with his hands in his pockets as he watched me walk away.

"I'll try to hurry," I said, growing more eager to be done with my responsibilities and free to hear what he had to say.

He shrugged again. "Take your time. I'm not going anywhere. I'll be here when you're ready."

With a quick nod, I rushed into the office and collapsed into my chair with my head in my hands.

"Are you okay?" Christine asked as she filed in behind me and shut the door. "Who is that? Have you been holding out on me?"

I took a few more deep breaths to calm myself before answering. "Yeah, I guess I have."

In the months after the crash, I'd been so emotional that I hadn't wanted to talk about any of it. The horror. The death. The fear. The heartache over a total stranger that made no sense.

I'd locked all of it inside and chosen not to share it with anyone other than Piper and my mom. And not even Mom knew the full story with Brick. I think she suspected there was more than I was letting on, but she hadn't pushed.

Christine, being respectful of my wishes not to discuss my ordeal when I returned to work, had only gotten the bare minimum of details.

I had no idea what to divulge now or how to explain who Brick was. What was I supposed to say? *He's some guy who saved my life a couple of times and who I thought might have been my soulmate, but then he left me?*

"Bri—uh, Michael and I met on the plane. He was one of the other survivors."

"Oh, my goodness," Christine said, her hand to her heart. "I can't imagine what the two of you went through together."

"Yeah, it was definitely a bizarre experience."

In so many ways.

"And he just stopped by? You didn't know he was coming? Is that the first time you've seen him since the...since you got home?"

I nodded, feeling a surge of anger and hurt that he hadn't even bothered to check on me in all this time. It was one thing if he didn't want a relationship, but common decency would have been to at least make sure I was okay once I'd gotten home. I tried to do the same for him, but with so little info about his life, I hadn't been able to locate a trace of him online. Obviously, he'd been capable of finding me.

"He wants to take me to dinner."

"Oh, well, that's nice of him." Christine came and sat on the edge of the desk, her smile almost a frown as if she wasn't sure which was appropriate. "I sensed some sparks there on his part. I'm not sure what I'm sensing on yours. You okay?"

"I'm fine. But I gotta get this stupid grant done and submitted by six or our mayor will have a coronary."

I had no idea how I was going to focus on numbers, projections, and percentages for the next hour knowing Brick was sitting outside waiting for me, but at the same time, I was thankful that I was able to process his return for a bit and mentally prepare for dinner with him. Several times I caught myself staring at the screen, my mind wandering down various paths of *what if* and *why*, but then I'd bring myself back to the task at hand.

It was seven minutes until six when I'd finally filled in all the necessary data and edited the passages to fit within the word count limits, and I hit submit with a loud exhale of relief.

Then, I checked my hair and makeup in the dim fluorescent lighting of the restroom and put on a fresh coat of lip gloss. After popping a stick of gum in my mouth, I walked through the darkened library to peer out the front windows.

A huge black truck sat parked in the front row, and I released the breath I didn't realize I'd been holding when I saw that he was still there.

I unlocked the front door and walked toward his truck, and he got out to meet me halfway.

"Done?" he asked with a grin. "Hungry?"

"Yes, and yes."

"Where would you like to go?"

I waved my hand toward the one main street that comprised Cedar Creek's sleepy downtown area. "Well, as you can see, I live in a thriving metropolis where the options are endless."

"I spotted Barnacles Diner on my way in. If the crowded parking lot is any indication, it's a popular spot on Friday evenings."

"Yeah, if you're over fifty and partial to everything on your plate being fried in the same grease. We could go to Ray's. It's seafood, and it's a little ways out, but it's closer than going to Jensen or Lumberville, which would be the next closest towns. They both have more options than Cedar Creek."

"I'm up for seafood if you are. You want to hop in my truck, or would you prefer to drive your own car?"

"My director already left, so I need to lock up and turn on the alarm system. I'll just grab my car from the back and drive around to meet you here. You can follow me to Ray's."

"Sounds good. You need help? Locking up or anything?"

I shook my head and couldn't help smiling a little. "Nope. I got it. I do this every night."

"Right. Of course. Okay. I'll wait here then."

NINETEEN

When we got to Ray's, it was packed with an hour wait, which I suppose I should have expected for a Friday night, but I was too caught off-guard to put much forethought into a last-minute dining decision.

"You want to wait the hour or go somewhere else?" Brick asked.

Curiosity was killing me. I was dying to know why he'd come, what he wanted to tell me, and where he'd been all this time.

I couldn't wait any longer to get answers, and I wasn't sure I wanted to have the conversation we needed to have in a noisy restaurant filled with nosy people.

"Let's get something to go and head back to my place," I said, and though I'd wavered before suggesting it, as soon as the offer was made, it felt right. It would give us a measure of privacy to talk, and, well, do anything else we might happen to want to do, depending on how the conversation played out.

"So, how are you doing? Are you all recovered?" Brick asked once we'd placed our order.

We were outside on the restaurant's porch, surrounded by other waiting diners, and every few minutes, someone I knew would say hello or try to start up a conversation. One of the hazards and joys of life in a small town.

"I'm good," I said. "I still struggle with a bit of a cough in the mornings, and I don't have tolerance for smoke at all, but my doctors say there doesn't seem to be any permanent damage, so that's a good thing."

"Definitely. And the ankle?"

"Oh," I said, looking down at my ankle as I twisted it left and right. I'd almost forgotten it had been injured since it had been so long since I had any trouble with it. "It wasn't broken, just badly sprained, so I didn't need a cast. I was in the hospital long enough that by the time I needed to put weight on it again, it had pretty much healed."

"I notice you're wearing much more sensible shoes." He grinned as he pointed at my sneakers.

"Yeah, today, anyway. I still rock my heels. I just don't go hiking in them."

One of my mother's friends touched my elbow and said hello before asking me to tell my mom the time had changed for the ladies' brunch Saturday morning. I assured her I'd let Mom know and then turned back to Brick.

He was grinning at me with his head cocked to the side, looking so damned handsome it almost took my breath away. "Is there anyone in this town you don't know?"

"Hardly. I come from a big family on my mom's side. Everyone in Cedar Creek knows the Wards one way or another. My dad's family is from here too, so if they didn't know my mom, they know my dad. Or both. My brother and I couldn't get away with anything growing up. One wrong move, and someone had already told my parents by the time we got home."

"And were you a troublemaker growing up?"

"Not really, but I was always with my cousin, Piper, and she's like a magnet for trouble. I got grounded for things that happened when I was with her more than anything I did on my own."

"That doesn't seem fair."

I chuckled. "You're telling me! And Piper's parents never really cared what she did, so she never got grounded. I'd be stuck at home for something she did, and she'd be out!"

He laughed, and at first, it made me happy to hear him happy. But then my heart hurt with the memory of what it was like when he deserted me.

"Why didn't you call?" I asked, my tone suddenly serious. "Weren't you the least bit curious to know if I was okay? The last time you saw me, I was unconscious. And you didn't even want to know what happened afterward?"

He frowned and stepped a little closer to me, leaning in to talk so we wouldn't be overheard. "I sat in the waiting room every day that first week until I knew you were conscious and that your chances were improving. I checked in twice a day every day after that, until you were discharged and my connection with you was severed."

"What?" My mouth dropped open in stunned disbelief and confusion. "No one ever told me you were in the waiting room. No one told me you called."

Shaking his head, he looked down at his hands. "I didn't want you to know I was there. I'd convinced myself you were better off without me, and I didn't trust my own willpower if I saw you again." His eyes met mine, the clear blue dark with sadness. "I couldn't let you go, but I couldn't risk wanting to keep you either."

"Who gave you updates? I know my family wouldn't do that, and the hospital staff aren't supposed to release information about patients without consent."

He looked away and then back to me. "Let's just say I'm very skilled at getting people to tell me what I need to know. And rest assured, I was never given any details. I just wanted to know if you were okay. If you were improving."

"You paid someone off?"

"No. Although I would have, if that's what it took. I just simply explained why it mattered to me, and why I couldn't ask for myself."

Before I could delve into what that meant exactly, the buzzer in my hand went off, indicating our order was ready.

I gathered the containers, and we went back to our vehicles for Brick to follow me to my apartment.

As I drove, my mind spun, struggling to process the new information I'd gotten. He hadn't deserted me. Not completely. He had been concerned about me, and he'd sought information while still trying to protect me from...him.

So why come now? Why go to those lengths to stay away from me and have no contact for months, only to turn up now out of the blue?

These were the answers I most wanted, and by the time we'd stepped inside my apartment, my patience had begun to run out.

"This is a nice place," he said as he looked around the small space I called home. "It's cozy. It fits you. Your personality. I like it."

I set the plastic takeout bags of food on the table and stared up at him, my hand on my hip.

"Why are you here?"

"I'm not trying to avoid the question, but it's a long story. Did you want to eat first?"

"No. I want to know why you're here. You told me seven months ago that you were no good for me. That you didn't have room in your life for me. Or for anyone. And now you just show up on a Friday night, and I'm supposed to sit here and eat boiled shrimp and coleslaw and corn on the cob and pretend this doesn't hurt like hell?"

"I never meant to hurt you, Lauryn."

"Yeah, well, you did. As if it wasn't already enough to deal with all the emotional crap that comes with surviving a damn airplane crash, you added this extra layer of pain and confusion that made it even harder. It would have helped to be able to discuss what happened with someone I went through it with, you know? Someone who was there. My parents tried to understand, and so did my cousins. But you lived it with me. You could have been an amazing resource for me in processing what happened. We could have been there for each other. But instead, you abandoned me."

"I thought I was doing—"

"And maybe it was wrong of me to think that some brief encounter that lasted less than twenty-four hours might mean something, but it meant something to me. And when you left, it hurt. It was like some weird breakup, but I couldn't even tell anyone that I was going through it because who was going to understand that my heart was shattered by some guy I knew for a matter of hours? Some guy I made out with while I was half out of my mind with exhaustion, terror, smoke damage, a messed-up ankle, and God only knows how many different psych issues from what I'd just been through and witnessed? I get that what I felt for you was probably not real. Hell, how could it be? But the pain was real. The hurt I experienced was real."

He rushed forward and took me in his arms, crushing my lips beneath his. With one hand in my hair and the other on my back, he held me to his chest as his mouth reclaimed me and made me see the folly of ever thinking our attraction was anything less than explosive.

"It was real," he whispered against my mouth as he pulled back just enough to look down into my eyes, still holding me tightly in his arms. "I'm sorry I hurt you, and I'm sorry I left the way I did. But please don't ever doubt that what we felt for each other...that what I feel for you now...is real. It's something more powerful and more real than anything I've ever experienced."

"Then where have you been all this time?" I dropped my fists onto his biceps as I stared up at him. "And if you were no good for me then, why come back now? You were so certain you'd make me miserable and that we'd be no good together. So, why are you here?"

"You asked me if my life made me happy. Do you remember that?"

"Vaguely."

"Well, I think to be more specific, you asked if I enjoyed my lifestyle. I'd never really thought about it before." He released me and paced across to the other side of my tiny living room. "When my mother died, I made a promise that I'd avenge her by making sure a debt was paid for what was done to her."

"And you did that."

"Yes, I did. And then I thought about all the other scumbags getting away with equally horrible acts, and I appointed myself the enforcer of justice for them as well. But I never thought about whether or not that made me happy. It wasn't even a consideration."

"Because it was your mission," I said when he paused.

"Right. But after the crash, after *you*...I don't know. They say when you have a near-death experience, you rethink your priorities and make changes in your life. I've had more near-death experiences than I care to count, and I definitely should have died more than once. Always before, I'd just get back up and keep on trucking, sometimes even begrudging the fact that I was still here. But this time was different. This time I actually thought about my life—my time here on earth—and how I spend it. I realized I want more out of life than just revenge and anger. I want to live rather than just avoid dying. I want joy and happiness in my life. I want to experience the kind of love my parents had for each other, and when I do die, I want to look back and feel like I lived in such a way that they'd be proud of the man I was."

I walked over and laid my hand on his chest. "I'm sure they're proud of you now, but everyone deserves happiness, Bri—*Michael*. That will take some getting used to. What made you change your name? Again?"

"Kind of the same thing," he said, wrapping his arms around my waist. "When I was a kid, I was Mike, Jr., my dad's pride and joy. Everyone said I was his spitting image. His miniature twin. And when he died, I was so happy I was a junior and I could keep him going, you know? But then when things started happening with my mom, when she was getting hurt by that jerk, Paul, I couldn't protect her. I felt ashamed that I wasn't living up to who my dad was and what he would have done if he were alive."

"But you were a kid! What could you have done?"

"I don't know," he said, releasing me to walk across the room again. "I did try to stand up to him, but Paul was easily twice my size back then, and he'd use his fists on me just as easily as he did her. Then when he...when she...when she died, I felt like my dad would never forgive me. I refused to be called Mike, Jr., after that, and when I went into the academy and the guys started calling me Brick, I latched onto it. I could embrace being this Brick guy, because then I didn't have to feel like I was letting anyone down."

He leaned back against my table and crossed his arms as he looked to me. "When I got back home after what happened with us, I got Kirby squared away, and then I took care of the cases I was already contracted for, but I didn't book any new ones."

A shudder ran over me at the memory of an arm around my neck and a shiv in my side. "Kirby! I wondered what happened with him. Did he go back to jail?"

Michael nodded. "Yeah, but he was offered a plea deal for the information he gave them, so his sentence was shortened."

"Okay, sorry—please continue. So, if you didn't book any new cases, what did you do instead?"

"Do you mind if I grab a hushpuppy? My stomach is growling."

"No, not at all. We can eat. Here, let me get everything out." I unpacked the food, handing him a hushpuppy before retrieving plates from the kitchen and divvying out shrimp and corn.

"I don't think I told you this before," he said as he munched on a hushpuppy, "but when my mother died, I went to live with my paternal grandmother in South Carolina, who did the best she could to steer me straight. She's the wisest person I know, and we've always been close. She's never really approved of the way I was living. I mean, you know, since I left the force." He peeled a shrimp and popped it in his mouth, and once he'd chewed and swallowed it, he continued. "So, I went back home to her, and I told her I knew I needed to do things differently."

"What did she say?" I asked as I filled my fork with coleslaw.

"Nothing she hasn't said before, but I actually listened this time.

She said I've been punishing myself just as much as the deadbeats I hunt down. That I have a problem feeling worthy of love and happiness, and until I decide I deserve both, I'll keep running and keep shunning any chance of having either."

"Wow," I said, nodding with raised eyebrows. "She does sound like a wise lady. What are you going to do with that?"

"Well, I set about trying to make myself a man that my family could be proud of again. A man who could carry my father's name with his head held high and look at my mother's picture without feeling shame." He took another bite and chased it with a swig of tea. "I told you before that I preferred to function outside the rules, and the longer I worked without the confines of being law enforcement, the more I was willing to blur the lines between right and wrong and find a way to justify it. I no longer liked who I had become.

"I met with the chief, and he's helped me get on a better path. Since I was never formally discharged or reprimanded, he was able to get me my badge back and find me a spot on a different team. I'm learning to use the skills I got out on the streets to help myself and others be better at doing our job. I'm coloring within the lines these days, and I feel like my pop would be proud of the changes I've made."

"Wow again. And you're...happy?"

"For the most part, yeah, I am," he said with a smile. "I still have a mission, but I'm pursuing it in a healthier way, and while the schedule is still grueling, it's nothing like what I was doing before. I have more balance, which I value now and never did before. I'm learning to appreciate days off. Time off. Free time. Time to pursue hobbies."

"Oh really? And what hobbies are you pursuing?"

He took another swig of his tea and set the cup back down. "Nothing too exciting. I enjoy driving over to the beach and sitting on the sand to watch the sun set. I've picked up the guitar again for the first time since I was in high school. I bought a barbecue grill, and I'm learning how to use that. I'm socializing, which is definitely a new thing. You know, accepting invites from my buddies for dinner at their house and things like that. I've even had one small get-together at my new place. I've discovered that I *can* like being around people in small doses."

I smiled at him, my chest filled with warmth and happiness to hear that he was doing well. That he was happy. But I still didn't know why he was here. I knew what I hoped was the reason, but perhaps he was just trying to make amends. To find peace with the way we'd left things as he embarked on this new stage of his life.

"I'm happy for you," I said. "You seem to be in a much better place, and you've obviously done the work it took to get there."

"It's been well worth it. You know, I said I was happy for the most part, because something's still missing."

I inhaled and held it, trying to brace my heart for disappointment if his next words revealed anything other than undying love for me and a desire to spend the rest of our lives together.

TWENTY

"I told my grandma about you," he said, reaching to take my hand in his.

"Uh-oh. What'd you tell her? What'd she say?" I braced even harder, because such a wise woman would surely have told him it was ridiculous to pursue something that had only lasted a few hours.

"I told her I'd fallen in love, and that I wasn't sure I was worthy of the girl I'd found. That I didn't know if I'd be able to make her happy."

My heart thumped loudly, and my palms began to sweat, but I didn't dare pull my hand from his as he continued.

"When she got over her shock, she told me a story about her and my grandfather. Another one I'd heard before, but it had never hit home the way it did this time. My grandparents met at a soda fountain. He was seventeen, and she was sixteen. He told her the first day they met that he was going to marry her someday, but that he needed time to make himself a better prospect for her."

"Sounds like a guy who knew what he wanted when he saw it," I said, popping a hushpuppy in my mouth.

Michael nodded. "Yep. So, he got a job that took him far away,

He wrote her a letter each week, and when he'd saved enough money, he came back to town and built them a house. And then he came to my grandmother, and he told her that he realized no matter how hard he worked or what he achieved or built, he would never feel like he was a worthy prospect of her love. But if she'd give him a chance, he would always love her, and he'd strive to be the best version of himself he could be for her every day of their lives."

"And that did it? They got married and lived happily ever after?"

He did his one-shoulder shrug and grinned. "As happily ever after as anyone ever is. They had good times. They had hard times. She'd be the first to tell you they had times when one or both of them might not have been their best versions of self, but she says no matter what trials they faced, they were committed to the idea that what existed between them was special and it needed to be fought for and protected."

"That would make a great romance novel," I said, picturing his grandparents at the soda fountain with their lives stretching out before them.

He lifted my hand to his lips and held it there, closing his eyes for a moment. I had the strangest feeling that he was saying a silent prayer.

"Lauryn, I wish I could say that I'm a great prospect for you," he said when he opened his eyes. "Anyone who loves a cop will tell you it's not always easy, and I have no idea how things might be for us when the world's not falling apart around us. Hell, we may get to know each other and decide we're completely incompatible. In the past seven months, I've done all I can to become the best version of myself I can be. Partly because I wanted to look at myself in the mirror and not be disgusted, but also because I wanted to make myself a better prospect for you. I'm still a work in progress, and I may never figure out how to be one of those perfect heroes you read about, but I don't want another day to go by without you by my side. I believe what exists between us is special, and I'm willing to try if you are. Please give me a chance."

"Holy crap. Did you like write that down ahead of time and memorize it or something? I'm not even sure I know what all you just said. My head's spinning right now trying to keep up."

"Let me break it down for you." He leaned to cup my face in his hand and brushed his lips against mine. "I'm in love with you, Lauryn, and I want to see if we can make a life together."

"I'm in love with you too," I whispered, and then, I kissed him wholeheartedly, holding nothing back.

"Is that a yes?" he asked once we pulled apart to breathe. "You're willing to try?"

"Yes. But I gotta warn you. I'm not perfect either."

"No!" His mouth dropped open, and he opened his eyes wide, laying his hand on his chest in dramatic mock shock. "You're not? This comes as quite an unpleasant surprise. I feel misled."

"Stop!" I laughed as I playfully pushed him away, but he reached for me and pulled me into his arms.

"To the world, you may be imperfect, but you're perfect for me."

I rolled my eyes and laughed again. "Where are you coming up with this stuff? Did you memorize a bunch of Hallmark cards? Geez."

"What? I'm being serious," he said, even though his grin and the sparkle in his eyes told a different story. "I thought a hero was supposed to compliment the heroine. Is that not a thing?"

"Compliments are good if they're genuine. But when they're over the top, it's just nauseating."

"Ah. Good to know." His grin widened as he squeezed his arms tighter around me. "You see, I'm clueless with all this romance stuff. Thank God you're an expert and you can teach me."

"I'm no expert! It sounds to me like we both need to be taking lessons from your grandma. She knows where it's at."

"I told you, she's the wisest woman I know."

"I want to meet this grandma of yours. She sounds like quite a character."

"She is, and you will. I've already promised her that would happen, and you know I always keep my promises."

"But how could you promise her that? You had no idea how I'd react to you coming back. What if I'd been in a relationship? What if I refused to forgive you?"

"I didn't put a deadline on my promise, and I wouldn't have given up," he said, his grin gone and his tone serious. "I'd wait however long it took. All kidding aside, you are the one for me, Lauryn. I knew it from the moment I laid eyes on you. It may have taken me a while to accept it, but we were always meant to be together."

I stood on tiptoes to press my lips to his, ready to begin the next chapter of our love story.

CEDAR CREEK

WANT MORE IN CEDAR CREEK?

Welcome to the small town of Cedar Creek! This quaint community is home to a collection of recurring characters who interact from book to book. If you've enjoyed reading Volume 2 in Cedar Creek Suspense, check out Cedar Creek Mysteries and Cedar Creek Families. They both feature stories of love, laughter, family, & friendships, but the mysteries have the added elements of suspense, mystery, and a ghost or two! To find out more, visit

www.violethowe.com.

ALSO BY VIOLET HOWE

Tales Behind the Veils

Diary of a Single Wedding Planner

Diary of a Wedding Planner in Love

Diary of an Engaged Wedding Planner

Maggie

The Cedar Creek Collection

Cedar Creek Mysteries:

The Ghost in the Curve

The Glow in the Woods

The Phantom in the Footlights

Cedar Creek Families:

Building Fences

Crossing Paths

Cedar Creek Suspense:

Whiskey Flight

Bounty Flight

Soul Sisters at Cedar Mountain Lodge

Christmas Sisters

Christmas Hope

Christmas Peace

Visit www.violethowe.com to subscribe to Violet's monthly newsletter for news on upcoming releases, events, sales, and other tidbits.

ACKNOWLEDGMENTS

Heaps of thanks and gratitude to:

Jennifer (Anamitra): To my fellow goddess, thank you for your guidance and insight, both on the page and in the classroom. Your knowledge of terminology and procedures helped give Lauryn's experience plausibility, and your ability to lift up other women and help them see their own beauty and strength makes you a real-life heroine in my eyes.

Christine: Thank you for sharing your knowledge of a library's inner workings and what Lauryn's day might be like. And thanks for making this author feel like someone special. Your support makes my heart all happy. Here's to ice cream, tiaras, and Fifi!

Chris: Thank you for completely ruining my entire premise... and then helping me figure out how to make it work anyway. I appreciate your friendship, your support, and your guidance.

Michael: Thanks again for letting me pick your brain to figure out my character's crimes and for your service and dedication to protecting my community.

David: Thank you for helping a non-hiking non-outdoors person understand what it might be like to be stranded in the mountains, and thanks for the area-specific crash site info.

Lesley: Thank you for helping me figure out where the crash took place and for recommending an expert for the area. As always, you rock!

Melissa and Lisa: Thank you for taking the time to be an extra set of eyes on this one. I appreciate your support and your abilities.

Tawdra, Teresa, and John: Thank you for being willing to say what works and what doesn't and for always helping to make it better.

Lauryn and Eric: Thank you for listening to this crazy idea for a story after I'd just gotten off a plane and for helping with suggestions for how it might work.

ABOUT THE AUTHOR

Violet lives in Florida with her husband and their adorable but spoiled dogs. When she's not writing, Violet is usually watching movies, reading, or planning her next travel adventure. She believes in happily ever afters, love conquering all, humor being essential to life, and pizza being a necessity.

Newsletter

Visit www.violethowe.com to subscribe and be the first to know about Violet's new releases, giveaways, sales, and appearances.

Facebook Group

You can also find out about joining Violet's Facebook Reader Group, the Ultra Violets.

facebook.com/VioletHoweAuthor

twitter.com/Violet_Howe

instagram.com/VioletHowe

amazon.com/author/violethowe

bookbub.com/authors/violet-howe

THANK YOU

Thank you for reading Lauryn's story. The magic in storytelling is sharing the adventure with the reader, so thanks for taking this journey with me.

If you liked this book, then please tell somebody! Tell your friends. Tell your family. Tell a co-worker. Tell the person next to you in line at the grocery store.

If you really liked it, please consider reviewing it on BookBub, Goodreads, your favorite online vendor, or any other social media site you frequent.